LANDSCAPES IN OILS

by J. M. Parramon

Published by
H.P. Books
P.O. Box 5367
Tucson, AZ 85703
602/888-2150

ISBN: 0-89586-093-7
Library of Congress Catalog
Number: 81-82131

Publishers: Bill and Helen Fisher
Executive Editor: Carl Shipman
Editorial Director: Rick Bailey
Editor: Randy Summerlin
Art Director: Don Burton
Design & Assembly: George Haigh
Typography: Cindy Coatsworth, Joanne Nociti, Michelle Claridge

Notice: The information in this book is true and complete to the best of our knowledge. All recommendations are made without guarantees on the part of the author or HPBooks. The author and publisher disclaim all liability incurred in connection with the use of this information.

Published in Great Britain by
Fountain Press
Argus Books Ltd.

First Edition in English, 1980

Original title in Spanish
El Paisaje al Oleo
©1976 Jose M.a Parramon Vilasalo

Deposito Legal: B. 33238-1979
Numero de Registro Editorial: 785

ON THE COVER: **Vincent Van Gogh.** *The Crau Plain* (or *Market Gardens*).

CONTENTS

LANDSCAPES IN OILS— A BEGINNING _____

Let's begin our study of landscape painting in oils with a look at the Impressionist painters of the 1870s.

The Impressionist style originated in France. Painters of this school concentrated on the *general impression* of a scene. They often used bright colors. They applied small, quick brushstrokes to imitate reflected light.

Impressionists held their first exhibition in 1874. It was during the age of industrial revolution, of scientific and mechanical inventions. Progressive artists of the day painted dynamic impressions as reflections of their new society. They rejected academic rules regarding composition and rebelled against accepted methods of the day.

Their palettes carried a range of unusual colors. They often omitted earth tones and used techniques based on new color theories. They chose everyday subjects or themes.

We begin with Impressionism because it's a style that has greatly influenced art. It's especially appropriate to landscape painting. Im-

Camille Pissarro. *Entree au Village.*

pressionism is often a starting point for teaching landscape painting. It is the forerunner of many art trends and styles of the 20th century.

Lessons in this book are based on the methods of composition and painting used by Impressionists Claude Monet, Camille Pissarro and Alfred Sisley. We'll also study Postimpressionists Paul Cézanne and Vincent Van Gogh. The Postimpressionists adopted many Impressionist methods, but they were not satisfied with the results. So they developed the style further and pioneered different techniques.

I'll update these methods by applying them to contemporary techniques, formulas and experiences.

We are in an age of *experimentation and searching.* This is reflected in today's art by new formulas and styles, many of which pass quickly.

The methods used by the Impressionists are still used by many professional artists. They often use identical methods. Sometimes the styles are varied.

Paul Cézanne. *Chestnuts at Jas-de-Boussan in Winter.*

Terms

We must define several terms before we continue our study of landscape painting in oils. Definitions apply to words or phrases as they are used in this book.

Asymmetry—Lack of symmetry or balance. See *symmetry.*

Axis—An imaginary straight line. It can run down the center—or across the center—of your painting. You can measure from this line to position parts of your picture. Symmetry, or the lack of it, is measured from the axis. The axis can also be the *centerline* or *midline* of an object or shape.

Color Harmony—The *pleasing relationship* or *combination* of colors in a painting. *Luminosity of color* in the landscape must be considered, as explained on page 68.

Complementary Colors—These are colors that are *opposite* each other on the color wheel, shown on page 59. Used side by side or near each other, complementary colors produce *maximum visual contrast.* When mixed, they produce *grays.*

Cubism—School of *abstract* painting and sculpture that began in the early 1900s. Cubist art work is characterized by brushstrokes and shapes that are basically geometrical, especially *cubes.*

Diversity—Diversity means *variety.* There can be diversity in shapes, colors and positions in a landscape painting. Diversity can be used to make an impact on the viewer and arouse his interest. It encourages him to *look* at the painting.

Hue—A hue is a *color.* We refer to hues by the *names* of colors. *Blue* is a hue, as are *red, green, violet, yellow,* and so on.

Impasto—This is a painting technique in which thick layers of pigment are applied to the painting surface. The pigment appears heavy and rough when dried.

Intensity—A color's *strength* or *weakness* is referred to as its *intensity*. Pure color is highest intensity. Mixing other colors with a pure color makes it appear dull or slightly gray. This *reduces* its intensity. A dull or grayish color is said to have *low intensity*.

Line—This is the artist's fundamental tool. Line can suggest *mass, texture, light* and *shadow*. It can have its own character, from an irregular scribble to a smooth curve.

Mass—The appearance of mass is usually achieved with light and shadows, or by placement of shapes. Mass refers to *blocks* of light or shadow without respect to details. We see masses of a scene when we *squint* our eyes.

Plane—A plane can be thought of as an *imaginary* flat surface that extends an infinite distance in any direction. Think of a *pane of glass*. A pane of glass is similar to a plane. Two panes of glass that are perpendicular to each other would be on *intersecting planes*.

Spectrum—Sunlight can be separated into light *waves*. Light can be seen in its simplest forms when it is directed through a *prism*. The human eye sees a *band* of six colors. This band is called the *spectrum*. The colors are *red, orange, yellow, green, blue and violet*.

Symmetry—This is the balance of shapes and masses on both sides of an axis, line or plane. A painting is called *symmetrical* if it can be divided into halves that are similar in appearance. See *asymmetry*.

Tonal Color—This refers to an object's *actual* color—or hue—under existing lighting conditions. Tonal color is often referred to as *local color*.

Unity—Unity means *order*. We achieve order by combining all elements of a landscape—line, size, color, shape and position—into a *harmonious whole*.

Value—Refers to the relative lightness or darkness of a color.

Vincent Van Gogh. *The Yellow Chair.* A simple yellow chair provided great inspiration for Van Gogh. Even such a trivial subject was of great interest to this Master, who is known today as a Postimpressionist. This is one of his better-known paintings. His concern in this work was with structure and color.

*Lesson From Van Gogh
Landscape Subjects of
the Impressionists*

Claude Monet. *The Bathing Place* (detail).

Lesson From Van Gogh

I am a great admirer of Van Gogh. I am deeply moved by his painting and his life. In my opinion he is the greatest landscape painter of all time.

The story of Van Gogh's life provides an important lesson about choosing subjects for painting. He made his own discovery of color and light. He pursued his work even after he had lost his reason and was hospitalized. He continued to develop his art while in the hospital. There he produced the best paintings he ever painted in his life. Then he committed suicide.

"I think I did the right thing when I came here," Van Gogh wrote from the hospital of Saint-Remy to his brother Theo. "The change of atmosphere has done me good.

"Since I have been here, the abandoned garden, with its tall pine trees and high, untended grass mingled with weeds has provided me with material enough for work."

Vincent Van Gogh. *The Artist's Room at Arles.*

The garden was rich enough in subject matter for several paintings. Van Gogh found inspiration to paint even in that environment.

When Van Gogh was living in Arles a year earlier, he created a brilliant painting of his room. Only two chairs, a bed and a small table were included, as shown above.

Perhaps we can understand the problem of choosing a subject through the words of his predecessor, Eugene Delacroix. Delacroix wrote, "The subject is you, yourself, your impressions, your emotions toward Nature. You must look inside yourself and not around you."

This is what we see in Van Gogh—his emotions toward Nature.

One great innovation of the Impressionists was their preference for *common, everyday* subjects. They shunned studiously prepared paintings in which the composition was carefully planned, sometimes down to trivial details.

For centuries, landscapes had been painted in the studio from memory or from preliminary sketches. As late as the 17th century, Nicolas Poussin and Claude Lorraine composed landscapes with an

Camille Pissarro. *Place du Theatre Francais.*

Vincent Van Gogh. *Cafe at Night—Interior.*

Pissarro and Van Gogh cared little for the well-accepted, academic themes of their day. These artists established new traditions with *common* scenes, such as those pictured here.

obvious element of fantasy. They idealized the subject. Their paintings were more formal and classically structured.

In contrast, the Impressionists painted *themes* rather than subjects. They painted topics that were *living, spontaneous* and *natural.* They chose subjects for emotional impact, rather than mere pictorial value. They painted what they observed in real life.

There is an obvious lesson to be learned. You will have little difficulty finding subjects suitable for landscape painting. They are on the street where you live, in town, in a garden, field, beach or fishing port.

Van Gogh and the Impressionists emphatically expressed their indifference about what subjects were fit for painting. They painted trivial subjects—at least they seemed trivial then. These included a crowd of people and horse-drawn carriages crossing a city square, viewed from a balcony—Pissarro's *Place du Theatre Francais.* Or the interior of a cafe with a billiard table—Van Gogh's *Cafe at Night—Interior.* These are reproduced above.

It appeared as though all they had to do was set up their easels and start work. Their subjects were already there. But they had considered the shape and color of the subject before they started painting. They analyzed the composition. They chose the subject for its *composition* and were not overly concerned about *content.* It didn't matter if it was a handful of radishes or a bunch of roses.

The Impressionists were aware of three basic abilities that are helpful in selecting subjects. They are:

Knowing how to SEE
Knowing how to COMPOSE
Knowing how to INTERPRET

These are talents you can develop to help you select subjects.

The order of these talents is arbitrary. They blend and seem to occur simultaneously. The artist must judge the best framework, lighting, viewpoint, shape and color when he is considering a painting subject. He simultaneously imagines what he can delete, what he can emphasize, dominant colors he can use and contrasts he can accentuate. He is "looking inside himself." He is interpreting.

Landscape Subjects of the Impressionists _____

Many Impressionists and Postimpressionists had a strong preference for certain subjects. These subjects frequently recur in their works. We can classify these subjects as follows:

Roads or Trails Leading to Towns—These were the subject of many paintings, especially by Pissarro, Sisley and Monet. See figures A and F on pages 13 and 16.

Snow-covered Landscapes—The Impressionists showed a fondness for such scenes. They probably regarded them as the most forceful expression of light. Snow scenes were also a confirmation of their theories about color such as the blue color of shadow. See figures A and G on pages 13 and 17.

Landscapes with Rivers, Lakes or Ponds—These generally include reflections in water. This may be the subject most often painted by all the Impressionists, without exception. They probably regarded this subject as an opportunity to depict impressions, movement and reflected colors. See figures B and E on pages 13 and 16.

A

Claude Monet. *The Road in the Village.*

B

Claude Monet. *The Bathing Place.*

13

C

Vincent Van Gogh. *Restaurant de la Sirene.*

Urban Landscapes—The Impressionists and Postimpressionists painted streets, squares and boulevards of Paris, complete with pedestrians and vehicles. They depicted the city as a reflection of the age. This timeliness was an innovation. See figure C above.

Landscapes with Orchards, Flowers, Grass, Small Trees and Houses—This theme was an example of the *unpretentious subjects* favored by the Impressionists. It was not based on any composition studied beforehand, as in figure D on page 15.

Rural Landscapes—Scenes included mountains and vegetation, sometimes with views of the sea. In these paintings there are almost always some houses or small villages. The Impressionists painted many landscapes portraying natural scenery, especially woodlands. Cézanne was especially fond of such subjects, such as figure H on page 17.

Van Gogh was exceptional in his choice of subjects. He displayed

Camille Pissarro. *Orchard with Fruit Trees in Blossom in Spring—Pontoise.*

very strong personal preferences. Like his contemporaries, he painted water and reflections. But he never painted a snow scene. He painted the sea, the countryside and the city at night. He always tried to express himself in striking, vibrant colors.

Subjects most often painted by contemporary artists usually fall into three major categories.

Rural Landscapes—Subjects usually contain mountains and rocks, or houses and small villages.

Urban Landscapes—Scenes include villages, towns and especially city streets and squares. Markets, suburbs, old quarters and slums are often painted. So are scenes featuring industrial buildings and railways.

Seascapes—Favorites are beaches, rocks, mountains, ships and seaports, all with water as an important element.

E

Claude Monet. *The Bridge at Argenteuil.*

F

Alfred Sisley. *A Street in Marley.*

G

Paul Gauguin. *Breton Village in the Snow.*

H

Paul Cézanne. *Woods with Millstone.*

2 COMPOSITION IN LANDSCAPE PAINTING

Diversity with Unity
Organizing Shapes and
   Spaces
Composing a
   Landscape
Golden Section
   Principle
Balance of Masses
How to Portray Depth

Paul Cézanne. *The House of the Hanged Man* (detail).

There have been many attempts to define the art of composition. Henri Matisse said, "Composition is the art of disposing—in a decorative manner—the various elements available to the artist for the expression of his emotions."

A definition that helps us further was stated centuries ago by Greek philosopher Plato. He said:

> **Composition consists of diversity with unity.**

Diversity means *variety* as we use the term here. Unity means *order.* There can be diversity in shapes, colors and position of elements in a painting. Diversity can be used to make an impact on the viewer and arouse his interest. It can encourage him to *look* and then give him the pleasure of *contemplating.*

The artist must not overdo diversity so much that the viewer is disturbed and distracted. Diversity must be organized. It must have unity, or order.

These two ideas are compatible when we apply them to composition. We can state the principle in two ways:

Unity with DIVERSITY
Diversity with UNITY

Stated either way, the principle is important to composing landscape scenes. Let's examine closely what the artist can do to create unity and diversity in landscape paintings.

ORGANIZING SHAPES AND SPACES

Imagine that you are looking at a landscape like figure A on page 20. You are in open country. You can see a bell tower on a church surrounded by a few buildings on a small hill.

In the background there is a deep blue range of mountains. You can see a yellow patch of ground formed by fields of wheat at the foot of the hill. There is another hill with stones, bare earth and vegetation on the left. In the foreground there are stalks and branches of grasses and shrubs.

If you paint this broad panorama as you see it, the result would probably have too much diversity. It would distract the attention of the viewer. He would look at the church tower and the buildings, which are the principal subjects of the painting. But he would also look at the stalks of grass in the foreground, the buildings on the right and the hill to the left.

To create unity, it is vital to move closer to the principal subject. This is the first problem that we encounter when we seek unity with diversity.

How do you organize these elements in the landscape? How can you arrange these shapes within the space of your canvas? I will illustrate on the following pages.

Composing a Landscape

A

This is the landscape we have decided to paint.

B

Which part of the landscape is best? Just the church tower and a couple of buildings? This idea is dull. There isn't much of interest here.

C

We could eliminate the brushy foreground and concentrate on fields, hills and buildings. This still lacks something. The landscape is too expansive.

We have to ask another important composition question here: Should we *center* the church tower in the painting?

D

Or should we move it to the left?

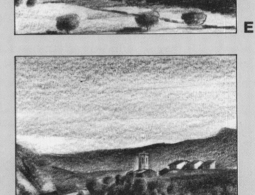

E

How would it look if we put the horizon and the church tower in the lower half of the painting? This would leave a large space for open sky.

F

We could go to the other extreme by painting church and buildings in the upper part of the painting. This would give more prominence to the fields of wheat. To see how I composed the final scene, see the direct painting exercise beginning on page 112.

G

There are no set rules to help you solve a composition problem. You have to rely on your eye. Consider the following principle when you are planning a composition:

Create a focal point in the composition.

We have a church, buildings, blue sky, bluish-green background of mountains, and fields of wheat. Choose a composition that includes these features and omits the rest. Eliminate the stalks of grass in the foreground. Reduce the large area of sky and the wheatfields. Get close enough to your subject to emphasize the church tower as the focal point. A common mistake of beginners is to paint great empty spaces, minimizing features that are essential subjects.

GOLDEN SECTION PRINCIPLE

Another principle is related to the location of various shapes within the painting, as shown in figures D through G on page 21. It is called the *Golden Section Principle*. For centuries this principle has been a traditional way of dividing spaces and arranging subjects in an artistic composition.

To divide a drawing surface according to the Golden Section Principle, the smaller part must have the same relation to the larger part as the larger part has to the whole.

There is an easy mathematical method to divide spaces according to this principle. You need only remember the number 0.6. Here's how you apply this method:

Multiply the width of the canvas by 0.6. The result gives you a dividing point within the canvas. Draw a vertical line at that point.

Repeat this with the height of the canvas and draw a horizontal line at that dimension. Where these lines intersect is a point that has traditionally been chosen for the location of the main subject. The diagrams on the opposite page help explain this procedure.

Measurements of this canvas are 24" by 18". To divide the space by the Golden Section Principle, multiply the width—24"—by 0.6. We get one space measuring approximately 14" and another measuring 10".

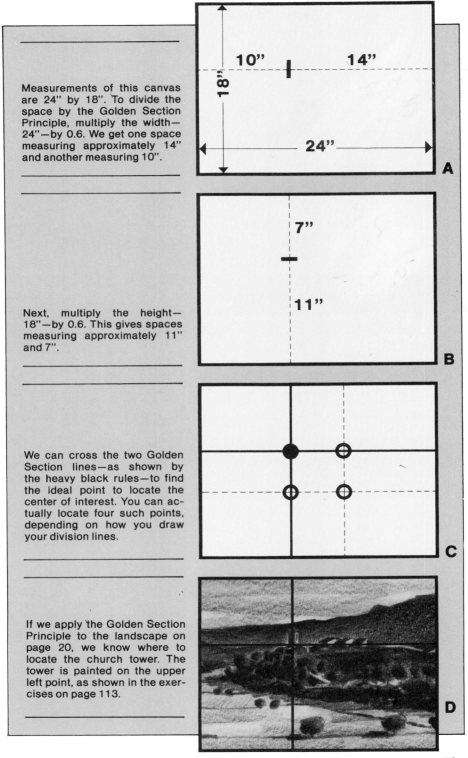

Next, multiply the height—18"—by 0.6. This gives spaces measuring approximately 11" and 7".

We can cross the two Golden Section lines—as shown by the heavy black rules—to find the ideal point to locate the center of interest. You can actually locate four such points, depending on how you draw your division lines.

If we apply the Golden Section Principle to the landscape on page 20, we know where to locate the church tower. The tower is painted on the upper left point, as shown in the exercises on page 113.

The Golden Section Principle is only one method of dividing spaces for composition. What may look correct and pleasing to one person may not be pleasing to another. It is a matter of personal taste. There are no rules. There is no "perfect" place to locate the church tower.

With practice, you can make this judgment without any mathematical calculations. You can learn to visually select the spot for the focal point of your painting.

SYMMETRY AND ASYMMETRY

Symmetry has much in common with unity. It expresses order, formality and authority, as in figure A below. *Asymmetry* has qualities

Symmetrical composition and direct front views of subjects are not the best methods when planning a landscape painting. Asymmetrical composition and an oblique viewpoint offer greater diversity and interest. The sketches on the left are symmetrical and frontal. They are dull and unartistic. The sketches on the right are asymmetrical and oblique. You can see the improvements.

common with diversity. It expresses movement, contrast and originality, as in figure B.

It is possible to control symmetry and asymmetry by moving the model in still lifes, figure paintings and portraits. In landscape painting the model cannot move, but the artist can. The painter can move around until he finds the best viewpoint.

Symmetrical composition is usually not suitable for landscape painting. It is usually more interesting to find an asymmetrical arrangement of objects. This means we need to paint from an oblique angle rather than from the front. Figures C and D illustrate this difference. Try to find the most effective angle that offers unity with diversity.

BALANCE OF MASSES

Let's analyze *balance of masses* in asymmetrical composition in landscape painting. Think of a set of old-fashioned scales. They have two weights at different distances from the *fulcrum,* or center point. These weights are kept in balance because one is larger and heavier than the other, as illustrated below.

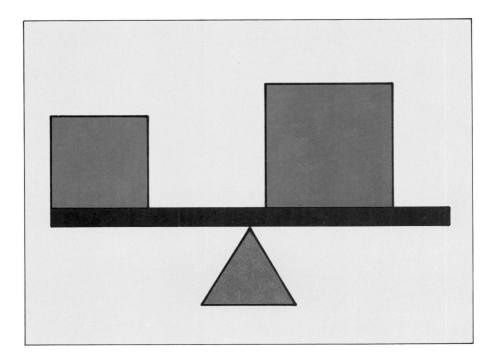

Camille Pissarro. *The Seine at Marley*. Pissarro chose a viewpoint that enabled him to balance the weights and masses in this scene. The scale in figure F and the block of masses in figure G simplify the elements of the painting. These demonstrate the balance Pissarro achieved.

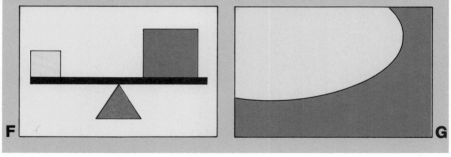

In asymmetrical composition, the fulcrum corresponds to the central axis of the painting. The weights correspond to *masses,* which are the large general areas of light or dark shapes. Figures E, F and G illustrate balance of masses in Camille Pissarro's *The Seine at Marley.*

Weight of masses must be compensated by others to achieve balance in a painting. Accomplishing balance depends on size, distance and value of masses.

In figure A above we see a group of houses, a few trees, a hill in the background and a grassy foreground. The scale in figure B shows that the mass of houses and the tree on the left are too heavy. They outweigh the features on the right. The result is an unbalanced composition.

In figures C and D the features on the left and those on the right compensate for each other. Balance is achieved.

You may object that although the composition in figure C on page 27 is better, it is no longer a true representation of the landscape. This may be a valid objection if your aim is realism.

The main difference is that the light comes from behind in figure A, leaving the group of houses in shadow. In figure C the light comes from the right.

It is also true that the trees are in different positions. Changes such as these are legitimate if they improve the painting. They are part of the process of *interpretation,* which I'll discuss more on page 42.

Figure E on the opposite page is another example of imbalance. The mass of trees on the left is not counterbalanced on the right. Relocation of features make a better composition, as in figure G.

Perfect balance is *not* always a decisive factor in composition. But it is worthwhile to keep viewpoint and direction of lighting in mind.

The following statement sums up the preceding ideas:

> **Changing the position of an element in a scene or finding a different angle of lighting can often make an improvement in the final painting.**

How to Portray Depth

The success of a painting sometimes depends on overcoming the limitations of a flat surface. A drawing or painting surface has only two dimensions—width and height. The aim of a painting is usually to reproduce three dimensions—width, height and *depth.*

In landscape painting, depth is an essential factor. You must make it possible for the viewer to "enter the painting" and walk along the paths, fields and streets.

The following are some techniques of composition to help achieve the *impression* of depth:

> **Include a foreground.**
> **Overlap planes.**
> **Take advantage of perspective.**
> **Emphasize contrast and atmosphere.**
> **Use colors that give the impression of distance.**

Let's study these techniques and see how they have been used in paintings.

A   B

Figure A illustrates the need for something to show depth. A tree proves to be the answer in figure B. This helps the viewer judge size and distance of background objects. To include a foreground, it is usually only necessary to change the viewpoint by standing farther back or more to one side.

Include a Foreground—A prominent foreground subject in a landscape composition creates an illusion of depth. This occurs because the viewer compares dimensions of the foreground subject with the size of distant features.

Suppose you have chosen a mountain village for your subject as shown in figure A above. The foreground consists of buildings and a field. The background consists of snow-covered mountains. But this arrangement does not sufficiently emphasize the *sense of depth.*

Let's change the viewpoint slightly. We can include a tree in the near foreground, as shown in figure B. This makes a great difference! The sense of depth is emphasized. A viewer will compare sizes and perceive distances. The viewer gets the feeling that he can walk from the tree to the houses and beyond.

Including a foreground such as this is a simple, classic method of composing a landscape. The Impressionists often used this technique. Figures C and D show two examples of how foreground subjects were used to emphasize the sense of depth.

Camille Corot. *The Bridge at Nantes.*

Look closely at these two paintings. The artists have emphasized the appearance of depth by including dramatic foregrounds. The trees and edge of the river serve this purpose in Corot's painting. A tree, a human figure and a boat make up the foreground in Monet's well-known masterpiece.

D

Claude Monet. *The River.*

31

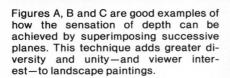

Figures A, B and C are good examples of how the sensation of depth can be achieved by superimposing successive planes. This technique adds greater diversity and unity—and viewer interest—to landscape paintings.

Figures D and E simplify the compositions of Monet's and Pissarro's paintings on the opposite page. Interest in these paintings is heightened by the use of superimposed planes. Study these to see how the sensation of depth was achieved.

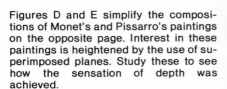

Overlap Planes—Let's place a series of buildings in a horizontal plane, one beside the other, as shown in figure A. The result lacks a sense of depth.

We can angle the plane and place some buildings closer and others farther away, as in figure B. We have achieved a partial sense of depth. This is because of the effects of perspective.

If we overlap buildings—superimposing them in a series of successive planes—we will increase the sense of depth, as in figure C. This is done by emphasizing the foreground, middle distance and background. We have created the *illusion of distance.*

This is a traditional technique. The Impressionists used it often. The two sketches—figures D and E—show in simplified form how the technique was used in the two paintings on the opposite page.

Claude Monet. *Snow Effect at Betheuil.*

Camille Pissarro. *The Red Roofs.*

A

Camille Corot. *The Road to Sevres.*

B

Camille Pissarro. *Lower Norwood.*

Take Advantage of Perspective—Camille Corot, Pissarro, Sisley, Van Gogh and Monet frequently made use of perspective. This increased the illusion of depth in their paintings. Corot and Pissarro preferred such scenes as a road that began in the foreground and ran into the distance. Figures A and B above illustrate their methods.

Sisley often painted houses and streets, as in figure C on the opposite page, and rivers with houses on their banks. He even painted scenes of flooded villages. Perspective was an essential factor in creating the illusion of depth. Perspective played a role in many of Van Gogh's and Monet's paintings, as shown in figures D and E.

C

Alfred Sisley. *The Road to Sevres.*

Claude Monet.
Roches Noires Hotel.

D

E

Vincent Van Gogh.
Montmartre.

A more detailed discussion of perspective in landscape painting begins on page 50.

Emphasize Contrast and Atmosphere—The German philosopher Hegel gave a good introduction to atmosphere and contrast in his book *Philosophy of Fine Art*. The following is a paraphrase of his remarks:

All objects undergo a variation in color because of the atmosphere that surrounds them.

The farther away objects are, the more they lose intensity of colors. Shapes become more imprecise because the contrast between light and shade becomes increasingly blurred.

It is usually believed that the foreground is the lightest and objects farthest away are darkest, but this is not the case. The foreground contains both lightest and darkest elements at the same time. This is because contrast of light and shade is most intense when closest to us. Closeness makes shapes more sharply defined.

Hegel's principles are important to landscape painting. Let's summarize his ideas:

Background objects lose intensity of color as distance increases. Blue, violet and gray colors dominate in distant subjects.

The foreground is more clearly detailed and has stronger value and color contrasts than distant objects.

You can see an example of these principles in the painting on the opposite page. The foreground—formed by two boats on opposite sides and by their reflections—are clearly defined shapes. There is a

J.M. Parramon. *The Port of Barcelona.*

group of boats in the center. The background is formed by the steamship and mass of sails on the right. Background color is less intense and tends toward gray and blue. Shapes are less sharply defined.

The idea of blurred outlines was expressed by Leonardo da Vinci during the Renaissance in his *Treatise on Painting.* He said that if the artist draws distant objects too distinctly and in too great detail, the objects will seem close. They should appear to be far away instead. Leonardo advised estimating the distance of each object and painting those that are far away without excessive detail.

Diego Velazquez was a master of this technique. He eliminated details, blurred outlines and emphasized atmosphere to create a sense of distance. Edouard Manet and Claude Monet visited the Prado

Claude Monet. *The Houses of Parliament.*

museum to study Velazquez' style. They were masters at portraying atmosphere by using blurred outlines of shapes. This sensation of atmosphere is exaggerated in some of Monet's paintings, as in the example above.

The illusion of depth can be enhanced by what I call *contrived contrasts.* Look closely at Cézanne's *The Bridge at Maincy* on the opposite page. There are contrasts that emphasize outlines of some objects in comparison with others. These contrived contrasts increase the illusion of depth.

In figure B—the line sketch after Cézanne's painting—note the circle A. You can see how the shadow edge of the tree trunk stands out clearly because of the value contrast with the background.

Paul Cézanne. *The Bridge at Maincy.* Cézanne knew how to make shapes and colors contrast, even if such contrasts didn't exist in the real subject. He accomplished this by using contrasting values, and light and shade to advantage. The circled points in the diagram show where Cézanne used contrived contrasts in the painting.

B

On the light side, the trunk is emphasized by the dark color of the background. Similar effects can be seen in other areas indicated by small circles.

Notice that these points are not a *realistic* portrayal of the subject. They have been *created* by the artist to *emphasize* certain shapes and distinguish them from others.

Contrived contrasts create the illusion that one object is in front of another, with space between the two. These artificial contrasts increase this effect even though the contrasts are not actually present in the subject. Leonardo da Vinci expressed the idea this way:

The background of a body should be dark on its sunlit side and bright on its shady side.

This statement can be simplified even more. For light subjects, paint dark backgrounds. For dark subjects, paint light backgrounds. The painting below helps illustrate this idea.

Leonardo da Vinci. *Leda.* This is a detail from Leonardo's famous painting. The landscape provides a background for the central figure. You can see how Leonardo painted dark values on the side exposed to light, and light values on the shady side. This effect is especially obvious in the hills and flat surfaces of the houses. Contrasts have been accentuated to distinguish and emphasize the shape and depth of some objects compared with others.

Use Colors that Give the Impression of Distance—When blue is painted next to yellow in a landscape scene, the yellow seems to *come closer* and appear to be in the foreground. Blue seems to *move away* and appear to be in the distance.

The basic principle is as follows:

Warm colors give objects the appearance of being close. *Cold* colors give objects the appearance of being farther away.

Colors listed below are arranged in relative order, according to how close or distant they make objects appear.

> **Warm colors are *yellow, orange* and *red.***
> **Cold colors are *green, blue* and *violet.***
> **Yellow makes objects seem *closest.***
> **Violet makes objects seem *farthest away.***

More guidelines for composing a painting can be found in *Composition,* another volume in the HPBooks Art Series. The book covers the basics of composition for artists, from beginners to experts.

Paul Cézanne. *The House of the Hanged Man.* The appearance of depth is enhanced by the warm yellowish and reddish colors in the foreground. This warm tone contrasts with the bluish colors of the distant sky. Warm colors help reinforce the feeling of closeness.

3 INTERPRETATION

Challenge of Interpretation
Three Methods of
  Interpretation
First Impression

J.M. Parramon's painting of a village street (detail).

Interpretation involves *changing something.* It involves *unique personal vision* and *opinion.*

For the artist, interpretation means painting a subject the *way he sees it,* not necessarily the way it *is.* He does not try to make an exact copy of the subject.

The artist interprets by considering his own unique ideas about the subject. He can modify reality when necessary to achieve his artistic aims.

Is it *right* to change shapes and colors of a subject? Is it right for an artist to interpret a subject in his own way? Purists who strive for total realism in painting may say no. But for centuries artists have supported the idea of interpreting a subject as they see it. It is the artist's way of expressing himself—his ideas and his visions.

Titian, Raphael and Peter Paul Rubens interpreted far more than they copied. Here is what some artists said about interpretation:

Eugene Delacroix—"Painters who simply copy their subject will never give the spectator a living sensation of Nature."

Marc Chagall—"We look on Nature as something routine in character. The artist must see it and paint it as something fantastic and fabulous."

Pablo Picasso—"The painter must mold in the painting his own internal impressions and visions."

Gustave Courbet—"I always paint in a state of excitement."

The artist often sees a landscape, *imagining* it already painted. He sees its shapes, colors and contrasts in his way. He *interprets* it. It has been said that *real* art constitutes interpreting, modifying and changing what is seen.

CHALLENGE OF INTERPRETATION

Interpretation is difficult because it involves the artist's imagination. We can't *teach* someone how to imagine.

Here are some helpful ideas about imagination and fantasy. Fantasy and artistic imagination involve the following three factors:

Ability to ANALYZE
Ability to COMBINE FEATURES
Ability to CREATE

Ability to Analyze—An artist spends a long time studying a subject's artistic potential the first time he sees it. He analyzes the framework, peculiar shapes of each feature and dominant foreground color. He compares them with those of the middle distance and the background. He studies the contrast of values and colors. The artist thinks about other images he has seen. He remembers their impact, their beauty or personal style. He may recall colors used by Van Gogh, shapes used by Cézanne or effects of atmosphere observed at another time.

He may remember the contrasts of a photograph in black and white. The ability to recall images while he is looking at the subject prompts him to *think*, to *modify reality* and to *make changes.*

Ability to Combine Features—The artist studies his subject and discovers combinations of *reality* and his *memories.* He thinks of fresh approaches. He emphasizes, accentuates, reduces or eliminates details. Then he reaches the stage of *creativity.* He interprets the landscape in his own way.

Ability to Create—Creativity now begins to play its part, based on the processes described above. It is the result of having a *fresh attitude* toward something you wish to *change.* The word *attitude* is important. It represents knowledge, thoughts and reactions. These are reflected as a desire to find a new approach to a painting. The painting will be different from present reality and from representations of the past. The ability to create leads to *originality.*

THREE METHODS OF INTERPRETATION

These are easy to remember. They are:

AMPLIFICATION—To emphasize, exaggerate or intensify an element in a painting.

REDUCTION—To diminish part of the subject in size, tone down a bright color or soften edges in the background.

ELIMINATION—To suppress, paint over or remove objects that detract from the painting's purpose.

FIRST IMPRESSION

Here's what often happens when you see a possible painting subject:

You stop, look, then look again, maybe from a different spot. "Wonderful," you think. "That blue background, this almost black

Jacques Villon. *The Little City.* Villon's city landscape is obviously not a *realistic* portrayal of the scene. But his *interpretation* has created a vivid, interesting painting.

foreground cut out like a silhouette. The houses in the background surrounded by a patch of bright yellow. What a painting this will make! It reminds me of the fields painted by Van Gogh. I'll paint that hill with four broad strokes of the brush and those bushes with black and green. I'll paint it almost without shadows. In full color!''

You ponder the scene in your mind. You become enthusiastic when you think what it will be like. You set up your equipment and grab your brushes. The painting in your mind is extraordinary. You begin to paint. You are in a hurry.

Half an hour after rushing into it like this, the painting no longer looks like what you imagined. It is just another painting. It lacks excitement.

What has happened?

Consider the explanation offered by French painter Pierre Bonnard. He said, "The basis of a painting is, in principle, an idea. This idea

Andre Derain. *Trees.* This study in contrast and composition is an example of *interpretation* carried to its full potential. The artist has combined elements of the landscape into a creative subject. He has painted a scene that conveys *his* idea of the landscape. Derain has avoided being excessively influenced by the actual scenery.

determines the selection of the subject and the painting itself. By means of it, the painting can become transformed into a work of art.

"This initial idea tends to fade away and give way to the visual image of the actual subject which, unfortunately, invades and dominates the painter's consciousness. When this happens, the artist is no longer painting *his* picture."

Bonnard admitted, "I have tried to paint directly from the subject, exercising scrupulous care. Unintentionally, I have allowed myself to become absorbed by what lay in front of me. I have ceased to be myself. I need, therefore, a very personal system of defense. I paint only in my studio. I do everything in my studio."

Monet was terrified of the possibility that a subject may gain control over him. He knew he would be lost if he spent more than 15 minutes being guided by what he saw.

Then how can we resist this temptation and seduction offered by the subject's *first impression?*

Cézanne may have had the answer when he said, "I have, in relation to the subject, a firmly established idea of what I want to do. I accept from Nature only what is compatible with my ideas, and the shapes and colors of the landscape as they are according to my initial conception."

We can imagine Cézanne looking at his landscape for a long time, formulating the idea that was to guide him. We can imagine him later repeating to himself when painting, "as I see it ... as I see it." He would never allow himself to be seduced by the subject's first impression.

IDEAS FOR SUCCESS

Success at interpreting landscape subjects is impossible unless you develop a thorough knowledge of art. This does not mean just the knowledge of history, names, dates and styles. It also means *remembering* paintings in museums, exhibitions, books and reproductions.

The *camera* is a helpful tool for learning how to select subjects and plan compositions. Take plenty of photographs for your files.

It is also helpful to keep a *clip file* of newspaper and magazine photographs for reference.

Follow the advice Picasso gave Genevieve Laporte when she asked him what she should do to learn how to paint. He said:

"You want to be an artist? Then *observe.* Observe what is going on around you. Take in the *effects of light and shade, patches and contrasts of color.* These are all potential paintings that you can remember when you start to paint a landscape."

4 TECHNICAL ASPECTS OF LANDSCAPE PAINTING

Boxing Up for Drawing
Understanding Perspective
Color Values—Light and
  Shade
Intensificationist Style
Chromatist Style

Claude Monet. *Regatta at Argenteuil* (detail).

I have taught painting to hundreds of students. One absurd notion I have encountered is that *drawing* is a *worthless* activity, while *painting* is something *sublime* and *poetic*.

Some students give up drawing as soon as possible. They turn out to be complete failures when they try to paint.

Van Gogh emphasized the importance of drawing in these remarks to his brother Theo:

"There are laws governing proportion, light and shade, and perspective, and they are vital to any painter. If you do not possess this knowledge, you are involved perpetually in a fruitless struggle and will never succeed in giving birth to a work of art."

In this chapter I will discuss principles of drawing that you can use in landscape painting in oils.

BOXING UP FOR DRAWING

Cézanne believed that every object can be reduced to the shape of a cube, cone, cylinder or sphere. Much of his work reflects this belief. Cézanne was setting examples for the *Cubist style*.

A house essentially has the shape of a cube. The trunk and the limbs of a tree can be reduced to a series of cylinders. The top of a tree, a bush or a pile of straw are all basically the form of a sphere, as shown in figure A below.

An expert draftsman does not draw cubes, cylinders or spheres. But these shapes are present in his mind as a basis for constructing and painting various objects.

This brings us to the process of *boxing up.*

The *proportion* of certain features compared with others can be determined more easily if you begin by drawing boxes or cubes. These represent various shapes, as shown in figure B on page 50. Actual shapes can be drawn in these boxes when proportions have been decided, as in figure C.

The HPBooks Art Series volume titled *Drawing* covers this subject in more detail.

A

Drawing any object can be aided by first sketching—or at least visualizing—one of three elemental shapes: cubes, cylinders or spheres. The drawings above illustrate this simple approach. This practice helps define shapes accurately and in proper proportions.

B

C

Boxing up helps determine relative proportions and shapes. When rough boxes are complete, the drawing can be finished, as shown above.

UNDERSTANDING PERSPECTIVE

Every artist who wants to paint realistic landscapes in oils must have a basic knowledge of perspective.

Perspective is the drawing technique used to portray three-dimensional objects on a flat surface. Perspective shows *depth* because edges of objects are drawn so they slant toward a common point in the background.

The roof edge and imaginary lines formed by balconies and stairs on a house will meet at a common point in the distance. This is called a *vanishing point.*

Here's another example. Pretend you are looking down the railroad tracks into the distance, as in the drawing above. The tracks and overhead power lines appear to converge at a single point as they recede. This is a *perspective view* of the scene. Objects must be drawn in this manner to appear realistic. Perspective gives the appearance of depth.

Perspective drawing is the subject of another book in the HPBooks Art Series. It is titled *Perspective*. The book includes a complete study of perspective for students and advanced artists.

COLOR VALUES—LIGHT AND SHADE

The Impressionists made an impact with paintings filled with light and color. Since that time, painters generally have been divided into two major categories:

CHROMATISTS—Painters who portray volume of objects by means of color. They make only limited use of light and shadows.

INTENSIFICATIONISTS—Painters who use color but portray volume of objects through heavier emphasis of light and shadow. They use actual, observed colors and shadows to determine proportions of objects.

Chromatists give priority to color rather than draftsmanship. Intensificationists are content to draw the subject as it is. It depends on the temperament of the artist. His temperament will be reflected in his style.

Van Gogh was definitely a chromatist. Salvador Dali is a skillful intensificationist.

INTENSIFICATIONIST STYLE

To *intensify* a painting means to portray different color values of a subject with different strengths of color.

Let's take a red poppy as an example. There is red in the poppy as we see it in the light. And there is a *darker* red that represents the *shadow* side of the poppy. To portray these two values of red is to paint in the intensificationist style.

The *intensificationist* painter concerns himself with light and shadow. This illustration shows the five types of lighting or shadow that the artist must paint. Color alone is not enough to portray scenes in the intensificationist method.

The artist must also distinguish between *real* shadow and *projected* shadow, as shown in the oil sketch above.

Maximum effects of light and shade are achieved by combining *partial front lighting* with *partial side lighting.*

Two other characteristics of light affect the intensificationist style — *quality* and *quantity.*

Quantity of light is influenced by the time of day. The artist may paint at noon with intense light or at dusk with subdued light.

Quality of light depends on atmospheric conditions. Light on a clear day is brighter than light on a cloudy, hazy, rainy or dusty day.

Quantity and quality have a strong effect on color contrasts. Bright light on a clear day will produce extreme color contrasts. On a hazy day, contrasts may be less extreme, or even non-existent.

Concern with color values and contrasts is the essence of the intensificationist painting style.

CHROMATIST STYLE

Is it possible to paint a landscape without shadows? Can the volume of objects be represented without emphasizing light and shade?

The answer is yes. Here's why:

Color separates and emphasizes shapes of objects.

We could paint a scene in black, white and shades of gray—without shadows—as shown in figure A below. But it would be difficult to distinguish between the reddish house, green areas and brown path.

These colors represented as gray are too similar.

A   **B**

The scene can be painted in full color—as shown in figure B—and objects are well-defined. Even without attention to shadows, shapes are clear. Positions are evident. Volume is obvious. This is the chromatist approach to painting.

Chromatist painting is most successful under the following lighting conditions, which reduce or eliminate most shadows:

Front or near-front lighting when the sun is bright.

Diffused or subdued light, as on a cloudy, hazy or rainy day.

Claude Monet. *Regatta at Argenteuil.* Monet's chromatist technique in this landscape involves the use of color without shadows.

Vincent Van Gogh. *The Crau Plain* (or *Market Gardens*). Broad strokes of bright color and dark lines to outline shapes are typical of Van Gogh's painting style.

Quantity and quality of light are not so important to the chromatist, compared to the intensificationist. The chromatist has little concern for shadows and contrasts.

Monet and Van Gogh paintings above illustrate the chromatist technique. Lighting is from the front. There are practically no shadows. Color alone makes the shapes stand out.

Van Gogh painted very little shadow. But he accentuated outlines and shapes with the broad strokes of color. Monet did not hesitate to emphasize parts of a painting with dark colors.

5 UNDERSTANDING COLOR

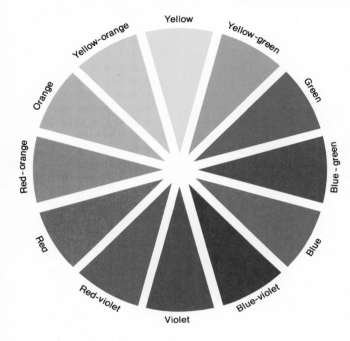

Mixing Pigment
Primary Colors
Secondary Colors
Intermediate Colors
Tertiary Colors
Complementary Colors
How to Gray Colors
Colors in Shadows
Color Harmony

Mixing Pigment

Color is one of the landscape painter's most useful tools. In this chapter I'll discuss the basics of color pigment and how to mix it.

The study of color can be divided into two categories.

Light Color—This involves sunlight or artificial light. Light can be separated into light waves. When sunlight is directed through a *prism,* the light can be seen in its simplest forms. The human eye sees a *band* of six colors, called the *spectrum.* These colors are *red, orange, yellow, green, blue and violet.*

Pigment Color—This involves the physical characteristics of artist's paint. Pigment color theory is the study of how paints are *mixed* and *blended* to be used in painting.

Let's study the colors and mixing theories that are the basis for landscape painting.

PRIMARY COLORS

There are three *primary* colors in pigments. These are the colors from which *all* other colors can be mixed—at least in theory. The primaries are *red, yellow* and *blue.*

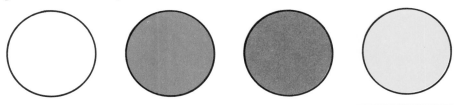

J.M. Parramon. *Landscape.* I painted this landscape using only three colors as primaries—Prussian blue, alizarin crimson and medium cadmium yellow, plus white. The result shows how all colors in Nature—even black—can be obtained by mixing these colors.

We think of the three primaries as *pure* colors. They can't be reduced to simpler colors. All other colors are the result of mixing primaries.

In practice, purity of these colors is only theoretical. This is because artists' pigments aren't actually "pure." Almost all pigments contain traces of other colors.

I have painted a landscape, shown on page 57, using only three primaries—*Prussian blue, alizarin crimson* and *medium cadmium yellow,* in addition to white. Study the painting and you'll see the broad range of colors you can mix from primaries.

It is relatively easy to mix colors for painting from primaries, despite their lack of true purity. Following are groups of colors that can be mixed.

SECONDARY COLORS

Secondary colors are produced by mixing two primaries together. The secondaries are:

Orange (mixture of red and yellow)
Green (mixture of blue and yellow)
Violet (mixture of blue and red)

INTERMEDIATE COLORS

Intermediate colors are those produced by mixing one primary and one secondary. The intermediates are:

Yellow-green (mixture of yellow and green)
Blue-green (mixture of blue and green)
Blue-violet (mixture of blue and violet)
Red-violet (mixture of red and violet)
Red-orange (mixture of red and orange)
Yellow-orange (mixture of yellow and orange)

Intermediates are actually secondary colors with an additional portion of one of the two original primaries added. The resulting color is dependent on the *ratio* of primary color to secondary color in the mix.

Let's take an example. If we mix nearly equal portions of yellow and blue, we produce a green hue—a secondary color. If we add more yellow, we are adding a primary to a secondary. We call this mixture an *intermediate color.* But it is merely the original green mixture— yellow plus blue—with a more yellowish appearance.

TERTIARY COLORS

Tertiary colors are the third group of color mixtures. We mix tertiaries by combining portions of *all three* primaries.

The color wheel below shows relationships between primary, secondary and intermediate colors. Colors that are opposite each other—or nearly opposite—are complementary colors—or near-complementaries. Complementaries are discussed on page 60.

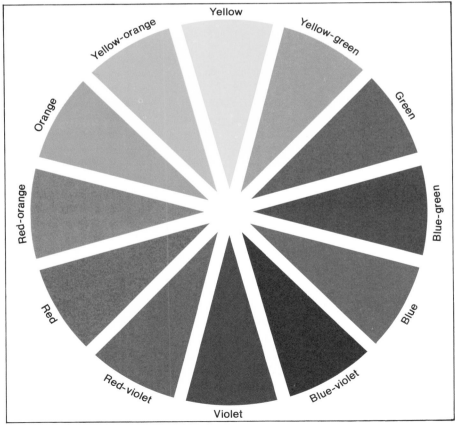

LEARN BY EXPERIMENTING

Mixing colors for painting seems simple—in theory—when we understand there are only three primaries. But there is only one way for the landscape painter to learn the peculiarities of mixing oil pigments: *experimentation.*

Color theories stated in words and on color wheels don't tell the whole story. Only practice with oil pigments on a painting surface can show you how to mix colors. Here's why:

Characteristics of colors differ from one brand to another. Also, *names* differ for similar colors. One brand's *cobalt blue* may have a bit more yellow in it than the cobalt blue from another maker. This situation forces the artist to learn practical color mixing by trial and error.

There are inconsistencies between *theoretical* color mixing and *actual* mixing of oil pigments. That's why few artists mix all colors from primaries. It is easier to select commercially made colors for your palette. This choice is the end result of trial and error.

Black and white pigments are added to the palette to give additional lightening and darkening capability.

We'll study selection of oil paints in chapter 6, beginning on page 71.

COMPLEMENTARY COLORS

In artist's terminology, we define *complementary* colors as those that are *opposite* each other on the color wheel.

To understand complements, look at the colors on the opposite page. These are the primary colors and their complements. A color wheel similar to the one on page 59 is a good reference for remembering complementary colors.

The use of complementary colors—or those that are nearly complementary—is important to the landscape painter. A painter can create *maximum contrast* between colors by using complementaries side by side.

Complementary Colors

The secondary color violet—a mixture of primary blue and red—is complementary to primary yellow.

The secondary color orange—a mixture of primary yellow and red—is complementary to primary blue.

The secondary color green—a mixture of primary blue and yellow—is complementary to primary red.

Maximum Contrast

Maximum contrast is achieved by placing complementary colors side by side.

There is a drawback to this kind of extreme contrast. Using vivid complementaries together can produce contrasts that are *excessively harsh*. These combinations are sometimes irritating and unpleasant to the eye. They may not give you the effect you want.

In other paintings, the use of complementaries and near-complementaries may actually be a desired technique. This is true when color clashes or contrasts are the effect you want.

The painting below shows how the Fauvist painters used this harsh method of color contrasts in painting. The Fauvists—who followed the Impressionists by several years—were known for their use of vivid colors, simple draftsmanship and rhythmic lines.

Maurice de Vlaminck. *Tug at Chatou.* A group of painters known as the *Fauvists* followed the Impressionists. The Fauvists were noted for their unusually bold, bright colors and distorted shapes. Their harsh painting style included the use of strong contrasts made by placing complementary or near-complementary colors together.

Graying Colors

Two complementary colors can be mixed to produce grayish-black. When mixed with white, the result is a lighter gray color. This type of gray can look *dirty*.

HOW TO GRAY COLORS

Another use of complementary colors is for *graying*. This technique can be both useful and detrimental to the painter. The difference lies in how careful you are.

Here's how it works:

When two complementary colors are mixed together, a grayish color is produced. This may be a desired effect. If you want to subdue a brilliant red, you can add a touch of green. If you need a grayish blue, you can add a bit of orange.

We also describe this graying effect as *neutralizing* a color. When we neutralize or gray a color, we *reduce its intensity.*

TRAP OF THE GRAYS

Mixing complementaries and adding an excessive amount of white pigment can lead to what I call the *trap of the grays.*

This practice can lead to dirty, gray colors that fail to give a landscape enough bright color. The painter can fall into this trap almost

A

I mixed the colors shown at left to produce ochres and green colors for this painting. Note that many of these colors are complementaries or near-complementaries. If I had mixed them in *equal* proportions and had made excessive use of white, I would have produced a totally gray painting.

without knowing it. Experience and careful attention to mixing can help avoid this pitfall.

The colors on page 63 show how mixing complementaries and white produces a grayish—almost black—color.

Complementary colors can be mixed in *unequal* proportions and white added to produce good colors within a soft, subdued range. The resulting colors are grayish but not dirty, as this example shows. There are no bright colors here. But we will get vivid contrasts that are *harmonized* through the use of complementary colors.

Successful mixing of complementaries and white depends mainly on the ratio of the pigments. Figures A and B on the opposite page and above illustrate this difference.

Figure B shows the excellent range of colors obtained by mixing unequal proportions of complementary colors. There is a rich variety of colors that are grayish but not *dirty.*

COLORS IN SHADOWS

A tendency when painting shadows is to add black or dark gray to the local color of the subject. The end result is darkness, grayness and dirtiness, but not shadow.

Black or dark gray implies the absence of light. In shadows—even the *darkest* ones—there is light.

Then what is the color of shadow?

The bright palette used by the Impressionists gives us a clue. They wanted to replace *pitch*—a type of dark color used until the 18th century—with the color *blue* when painting shadows.

Monet, one of the founders of Impressionism, observed, "When night falls, the entire landscape turns blue."

We know that *the influence of the color blue increases as light decreases.*

That's why blue is the most important color in any shaded area.

The second color in shadow is the color that is complementary to the actual color of the subject. If we paint blue in a distant mountain, the colors of the shadow will include orange. This color is complementary to blue.

The third and last color in shadow is a darker tone of the actual color of the subject. This *tonal* color in a mountain can be produced by mixing *blue* with a small amount of *burnt sienna* or *raw sienna*.

Here's a principle that summarizes how to mix shadow color:

Blue
plus
Color complementary to actual color of subject
plus
Tonal color

This landscape was painted to illustrate color combinations that produce accurate shadow colors. The painting includes a green tree throwing its shadow across a yellow ochre wheatfield. The mountain in the background is a bluish color. The list below breaks down the colors used to mix shadow color.

1—Shaded Parts of Tree	
Blue	Prussian blue, diluted with white
The color complementary to green	Red, slightly diluted with white
Tonal color	Green and raw sienna

2—Ground Shadow of Tree	
Blue	Cobalt blue, diluted with white
The color complementary to yellow	Ultramarine blue
Tonal color	Yellow ochre

3—Mountain Shadow	
Blue	Ultramarine blue, diluted with white
The color complementary to blue	Orange—very little
Tonal color	Cobalt blue with a touch of raw sienna

THREE BLUES ON THE PALETTE

In the illustration above we see the use of three blues—*Prussian blue, cobalt blue* and *ultramarine blue.*

It is not possible to recommend one blue instead of another in each case. The choice of appropriate blue depends on several factors. The most important factor is the *harmony of colors* used in the landscape.

COLOR HARMONY

Color harmony is the *pleasing relationship* of colors with other colors in a painting. To select harmonious colors, the artist must keep in mind the *luminous tendency* of the landscape. This is the luminous brilliance of colors in a landscape under certain lighting conditions. He must paint in accordance with this tendency.

The luminosity of Nature helps us achieve harmony in our use of color. Luminosity links some colors to others and harmonizes the entire range of colors.

Let's examine three kinds of luminosity.

Reds and Yellows—This luminosity occurs in bright sunlight in midsummer between 4 p.m. and 6 p.m. Urban landscapes are most affected. The luminous tendency is composed of yellows, oranges, ochres and reds.

Blues—A blue luminosity dominates on a sunny day in winter. This is especially true between 9 a.m. and 11 a.m. in the open country and even more in mountainous country.

Grays—Color tendency is gray on a cloudy day in rural country and in the city. Grays are produced by the mixture in unequal proportions of complementary colors. Figure B on page 65 illustrates the gray tendency.

The process appears simple. The artist has to identify the luminous tendency and then interpret it in his painting.

But there's a problem here for the artist. The luminous tendency is not always as easy to identify as in the three preceding examples. The solution is to make a decision and select one of the three color ranges. Then begin painting with confidence.

WARM COLORS

A *color range* is a succession of colors in order. The term *warm range* is applied to hues of red, orange and yellow. It stretches from yellow-green to red-violet on the color wheel, as shown on the opposite page.

Warm and Cold Colors

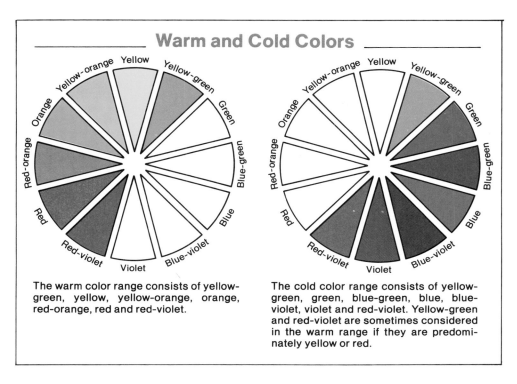

The warm color range consists of yellow-green, yellow, yellow-orange, orange, red-orange, red and red-violet.

The cold color range consists of yellow-green, green, blue-green, blue, blue-violet, violet and red-violet. Yellow-green and red-violet are sometimes considered in the warm range if they are predominately yellow or red.

Painting with a warm color range does not mean exclusively using these colors. It means painting with all colors while making the warm ones *dominant.*

COLD COLORS

The *cold range* of colors includes blue and its derivatives. Greens and violets are the halfway point between warm and cold colors. Greens with a yellowish tinge and violets with a reddish tinge may be classified as warm.

RANGE OF COMPLEMENTARY COLORS

A *complementary color range* is produced by mixing complementaries in unequal proportions as explained in figures A and B on pages 64 and 65.

When painting in soft, grayish colors, the artist uses other colors as well. But the goal is to obtain subdued colors and values. Some vivid colors can be used. They should not be as strong as when they are fresh and unmixed from the tube.

Oil Paints Used in Landscape Painting

Lemon Yellow	Burnt Umber	Viridian
Medium Cadmium Yellow	Vermilion	Ultramarine Blue
Yellow Ochre	Alizarin Crimson	Cobalt Blue
Burnt Sienna	Light Green	Prussian Blue

Titanium White and Ivory Black should be added to this list.

MATERIALS AND EQUIPMENT 6

Oil Pigments
Brushes
Palette Knives
Painting Surfaces
Palette
Thinners
Cups, Rags and Boxes
Painting Easels
Chairs, Carriers

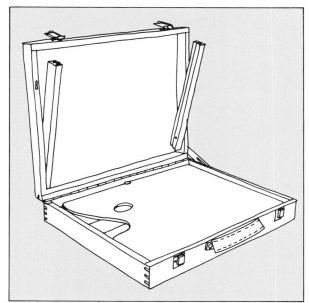

Good-quality oil paints are necessary for good painting. The following are all quality oil paint brands—Talens, Bellini, Shiva, Permanent Pigments, Bocour, Winsor Newton and Grumbacher.

Paints are usually available in two grades—*student* and *artist*. Student colors are less expensive and not as high-quality as artist grade.

Choose a brand you like and get to know the colors. Experiment until you are satisfied with your choices.

A more detailed discussion of oil painting equipment is found in the HPBooks Art Series volume titled *Oils*.

OIL PIGMENTS

A typical range of colors would match the color chart on the opposite page.

You can eliminate lemon yellow, burnt sienna and ivory black if you wish to reduce this selection. But you may find it helpful to work with the complete palette.

White is the color most frequently used. It is advisable to keep a large tube on hand.

Oil paints are sold in tubes with screw tops. Each brand sells two or three different sizes of tubes.

BRUSHES

Brushes should be made of *hog bristle* or *red sable*. They are numbered according to size.

You'll want good-quality brushes with long bristles or hair. These are more flexible, hold their shape and last longer. Cheap, poorly made brushes will leave bristles on your painting as you work.

Bristle brushes will be your most-used brushes. They're strong and produce expressive strokes. These brushes work well for painting *backgrounds* and *large areas,* and for *stippling* and *shading.*

Sable brushes are the choice for a *smooth painting style* and for *even, flat coats.* They also work well for *outlining,* coloring *small shapes,* painting *fine details* and *lines.*

Brushes used for landscape painting are made with several kinds of tips. Each has a different shape and is suited for different brushstrokes.

Hog bristle shapes are *round, flat, bright* and *filbert.* Sable brushes are made in *round, flat, bright* and *long* shapes. The figure below illustrates each of these.

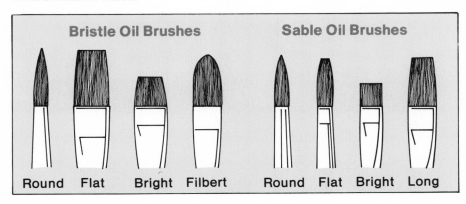

Bristle Oil Brushes — Round, Flat, Bright, Filbert
Sable Oil Brushes — Round, Flat, Bright, Long

Round brushes are best for painting lines. *Flat brushes* may be most popular. They can be used flat with broad strokes or on edge to make lines and outlines. The same is true for *bright brushes,* which have shorter bristles. I find the brights more suitable for smoother painting. *Filbert brushes* are more rounded or curved than a flat brush. Filberts are shaped like a cat's tongue. *Long sable brushes* are shaped like *flat hog bristle brushes.*

The number stamped on brush handles indicates the thickness of bristles or hairs. They begin with No. 1 and No. 2, then proceed in even numbers to 22.

Brushes Commonly Used in Landscape Painting

Two round bristle brushes — No. 4
Two round sable brushes — No. 6
Two flat bristle brushes — No. 6
Three flat bristle brushes — No. 8
One filbert bristle brush — No. 8
Two flat bristle brushes — No. 12
One flat bristle brush — No. 14
One filbert bristle brush — No. 14
One flat bristle brush — No. 20

The choice of flat or filbert brushes is optional. I prefer flat brushes because I think they make better brushstrokes.

PALETTE KNIVES

Palette knives are used mostly for four purposes:

Mixing paint on the palette.

Direct painting, instead of using brushes.

Cleaning a freshly painted area to correct an error.

Cleaning the palette after painting.

A palette knife shaped like a straight or bent stonemason's trowel is preferable for painting and cleaning an area. This type is *flexible*.

Use the knife-shaped type to clean the palette. It's more *rigid*.

Painting with the palette knife is discussed on page 119.

PAINTING SURFACES

Surfaces most frequently used for landscape painting in oils are *canvas, panels, cardboard* or *heavy drawing paper.*

Canvas is made of *linen* or *hemp* and is manufactured in various thicknesses. It is sold in various surface *roughnesses.*

Canvas is sold by the yard or mounted on wooden *stretchers.* Stretchers consist of a wooden framework with small *wedges* at the four corners. These wedges make it possible to stretch the canvas properly.

You can buy canvas, panels and cardboard with a *primer* or *coat of paint* applied on one side. Primer is a liquid coating that makes possible greater adherence and conservation of oil paints.

Canvas is sold primed in white, gray or sienna color. This provides a colored background that may be appropriate for certain subjects.

Wood or hardboard panels usually have a primer of glue and gypsum, offering a smooth, non-glossy surface.

You can buy cardboard—or prepare ordinary, good-quality, thick cardboard yourself with a thin coat of oil paint. This can be an excellent painting surface. The surface makes possible a completely *mat-finished* painting—which is a *dull* finish. This can be varnished when complete.

Thick, good-quality drawing paper is a suitable surface for painting preliminary outlines and sketches. It must be thoroughly primed.

PALETTE

Palettes are traditionally made in oval or rectangular shapes. They are usually wood, plastic or china.

Palettes have a hole in one end for your thumb. The end is shaped so one hand can hold the palette while you paint with the other.

Don't buy a palette until you've held it and judged how it feels in your hand, resting on your forearm.

Size of your palette depends on the size of your painting. Many painters have two or three palettes, from small to large.

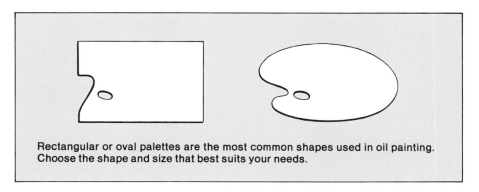

Rectangular or oval palettes are the most common shapes used in oil painting. Choose the shape and size that best suits your needs.

THINNERS

Thinners normally used in oil painting are *essence of turpentine*— which is *refined* turpentine—and *linseed oil.*

Essence of turpentine gives colors a mat quality. Linseed oil makes them more vivid. Essence of turpentine helps the oil paints dry more quickly. For this reason, it is appropriate for the rapid painting of landscapes.

Many artists use a mixture of essence of turpentine and linseed oil in equal parts. This gives the advantage of both thinners.

Keep a large bottle of essence of turpentine available. It is used more often than linseed oil. It can be used for cleaning brushes and your hands, although *ordinary turpentine* is preferred. This is explained on page 80.

PALETTE CUP

A palette cup is a small utensil with one or two cavities to hold thinners. Its base has a clip so it can be attached to the palette.

RAGS

It is essential to have a supply of rags to clean brushes, wipe your hands, wipe away part of the painting and to clean the palette.

PAINTING BOXES

The illustration on the opposite page shows the traditional equipment carrying case—called a *painting box.*

The box is made of varnished wood. It resembles a small suitcase as shown in figure A. The palette is attached to the framework of many boxes, as shown in figure B. There are two strips of wood inside the top that can be inclined forward. The strips have an internal groove for inserting a panel or piece of cardboard for painting. This is illustrated in figure C.

You can use this box for sketching and painting. The top serves as an inclined easel. The lid can be closed with the painting inside, where it is protected as in figure D.

The box is divided into compartments for storing tubes of paint, brushes, palette knives and other equipment.

OUTDOOR EASELS

The most common outdoor easel is a wooden tripod with folding legs for easy carrying. The easel should be light, strong, sufficiently tall and equipped to hold the painting steady.

In the illustration on page 78, models A and B are the most common design. Model A is simpler. Model B is larger, more solid and sophisticated.

Model C combines painting box and easel in one piece. This design is convenient and stable. It is compact when folded and easy to set up.

Model D is similar to model B, except that it is constructed of metal.

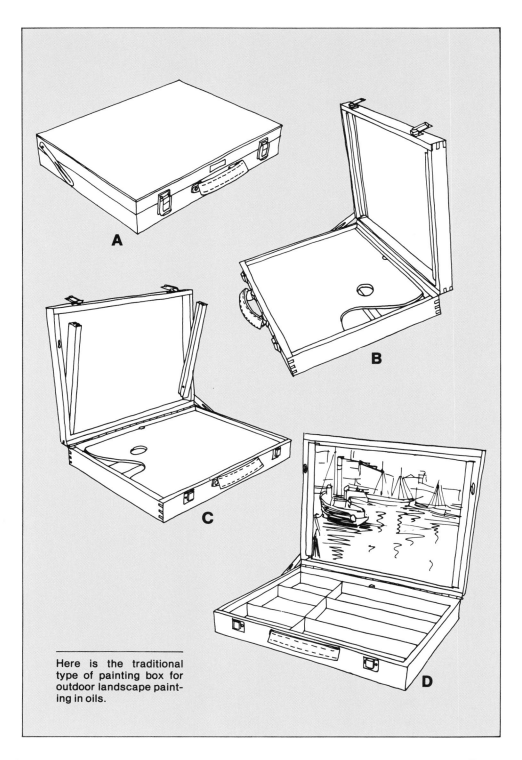

A

B

C

D

Here is the traditional type of painting box for outdoor landscape painting in oils.

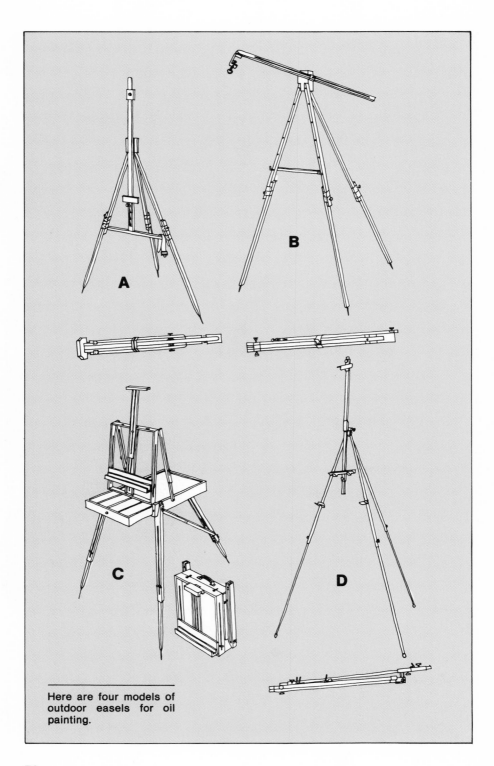

Here are four models of outdoor easels for oil painting.

STOOLS AND CHAIRS

You may want a stool or chair for painting sessions when you don't want to stand. I recommend a folding metal and canvas chair for maximum comfort. They are light, stable and compact.

STRETCHER CARRIERS

This simple, practical piece of equipment comes in two parts. It's used for carrying already-painted canvases. The most useful type is illustrated in figures A and B. This device holds two stretchers.

Some painters use four nails sharpened at each end and a soft substance in the center, as shown in figure C. These are used to temporarily nail together painted canvases, keeping them rigidly separated.

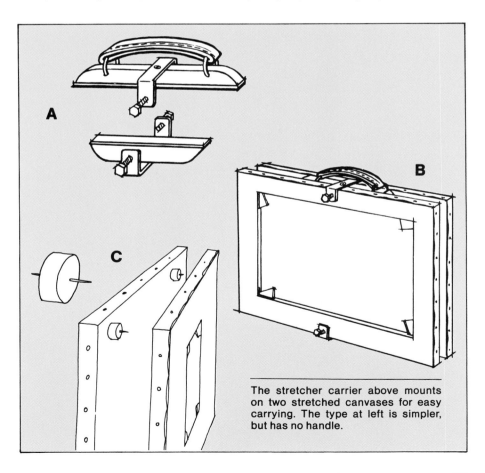

A

B

C

The stretcher carrier above mounts on two stretched canvases for easy carrying. The type at left is simpler, but has no handle.

7 HELPFUL HINTS

Here are some practical suggestions that will be useful to landscape painters.

Save Rags and Scraps of Newspaper—Rags and scraps of newspaper are useful for oil painting. Sheets of newspaper are good for cleaning brushes and palette. Carry a paper bag for your scraps.

Use Ordinary Turpentine for Cleaning—Include a small bottle of *ordinary turpentine* in your equipment. Use it to clean your hands, clothes, brushes and palette. Stains on clothes can be cleaned by rubbing with a clean cloth soaked in ordinary turpentine. Do this while the paint is still *wet*. This method is less successful once the paint has dried. Ordinary turpentine should be carried *outside* the painting box. When you finish painting, clean your hands with turpentine. Here's the best way. Open your left hand and put a clean rag in it. Squirt turpentine over the rag. Rub your hands with the rag until paint is removed.

Do NOT Paint with ORDINARY Turpentine—Ordinary turpentine can change the drying process of paint. Paint may crack after a time if you use ordinary turpentine as a thinner. For thinning, use only turpentine that has been *refined* and prepared for painting. This is called *essence of turpentine*. It's available in art supply stores.

Clean Your Brushes—This can be done entirely with ordinary turpentine, but there is a risk of brush hairs coming apart. The brush may eventually look like an old broom. Best materials for cleaning brushes are *soap and water*. Here's how. First, remove remaining paint from the brush with a rag soaked in ordinary turpentine. When there is practically no paint left, stroke the bristles against a bar of hand soap. Do this as if painting. Then rub the bristles on the palm of your hand. Rub backward and forward and in a circular motion. Don't twist the bristles. The soapy lather will be the color of the paint on the brush. This indicates the brush is still not clean. Rinse the brush out with water. Repeat the operation two or three more times until lather is white and brush is clean. Dry the brush with a rag. Store it in a jar with bristles upward.

Wear Old Clothes—Many artists wear a smock while painting. They feel at ease and less worried about getting paint on their clothes. An old shirt in summer or old sweater in winter will do just as well.

You Can Delay Cleaning Brushes—Brushes *must* be cleaned while paint is still liquid. Cleaning is extremely difficult and damaging to the brush if the paint has dried. Cleaning brushes may be the most tedious task in the painter's occupation. You can delay this chore until later if necessary. Keep the brushes *covered by water* in a shallow bowl. They will be protected for two or three days in this condition. Then they must be cleaned.

Don't Let Stuck Tube Caps Frustrate You—Caps on oil paint tubes often get stuck. This happens if the cap has not been screwed on properly and the paint dries. Don't try to force the cap open. This can crumple or break the tube. Light a match or cigarette lighter and *warm* the cap in the flame. Then unscrew the cap with a rag. Be careful—they get hot! Or you can use pliers to loosen the heated cap.

Save Old Canvases—Don't throw canvases away. Paint them with a coat of oil paint—*gray, beige* or *bright sienna*. This produces a canvas with a colored background that you can use. If the canvas previously bore an unsuccessful painting, its surface will still show dried clots and ridges. You will obtain a thick *impasto* impression when you paint on it again.

Alternative Palettes—A wooden palette—rectangular or oval—is usually used for landscape painting. Actually, *any* surface can be used as a palette. It has been said that Picasso never used a palette, but used newspaper instead. Matisse used a plate. If you misplace or forget your usual palette, use any disposable surface that is available.

Camera Can Be Useful—Take a camera with you when you go painting. Use it to record subjects while traveling. Keep photographs in a reference file. A camera can help you study and practice composition and select viewpoints. Use it to photograph the scene you are painting. Later, you can compare the painting with the photograph for retouching and adding finishing touches. Color photographs are usually more useful than black and white.

Music Helps While You Paint—Take along a cassette-player or portable radio when you paint outdoors. Music can be relaxing—or even *inspiring*—when you paint.

Carry Twine in Paint Box—Strong twine can often solve small problems—the carrying case that won't close properly, bundling small pieces of equipment or mending a broken easel.

Stabilize Easel in High Wind—Canvas mounted on an easel is like a boat's sail. Easel and canvas become unstable when the wind blows. This is another occasion to use your strong twine. Find a fairly heavy stone and tie the twine around it. Suspend it from the top of the easel between the legs. If the situation becomes unmanageable, pack everything up! Try painting on another day.

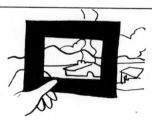

Select Composition and Viewpoint with a Viewfinder—This simple, portable device is good for studying composition and *cropping* your subject. It consists of a cardboard rectangle. It can be any size, but about 5x7" works well. Cut a hole about 3x5" in it. View your subject through this rectangle to study the best viewpoint and composition.

Select Viewpoint Using Your Hands or Four Paintbrushes—You can substitute your hands for the previous method. Place them in the position similar to the viewfinder. Or use four paintbrushes, forming a rectangle. When you are experienced, you can use only two brushes to form a right angle. You'll learn to see the composition without the help of a cardboard frame. When in doubt, establish the framework by one of the procedures described.

Wear a Hat When Painting Outdoors on Hot Days—A hat is often essential. Almost any kind will do. It will prevent sunburn and keep direct light out of your eyes.

Paint During Best Hours—Any time is suitable for painting on cloudy days. When the sky is clear and sun bright, best painting times are 9 a.m. to 11 a.m. and 4 p.m. to 6 p.m. Hours in the middle of the day are equally suitable if you paint in the *chromatist* style.

Don't Be Dazzled by Sunlight—There is a famous painting by Edouard Manet called *Monet Painting on the Seine*. Claude Monet can be seen beneath an umbrella. He's painting in bright sunlight on the deck of a boat. There is another picture of Renoir painting under a large sunshade. When the sun is high and bright, colors on canvas have a *dazzling* effect. The artist unwittingly employs a range of darker colors. His painting will appear dull when it is hung in a room with normal lighting. It is not advisable to paint in very bright sunlight. Paint in the shade or postpone it for another day.

Squint Your Eyes to See Masses—Look at your subject occasionally with your eyes half-closed. This blurs minor details and allows you to see main masses of shape and color. The technique helps you study shapes of objects. You can quickly analyze painting subjects. With eyes half-closed, you see large patches of color. Large masses determine your composition.

Learn When to Stop Painting—Do as boat oarsmen do. They put the oars into the water and row as hard as they can. Then they rest. You should do the same. Get up occasionally from your painting. Relax. Come back later. Try to see where you have succeeded and where you have made mistakes. Don't concentrate on one small area for too long. A painting is viewed as a complete picture. Each section must contribute to the whole.

Sign Your Paintings Like a Professional—Sign with a subdued color. Do not sign in vivid red or blue. Make your signature a discreet size. Sign in an inconspicuous place, usually in a corner of the painting. If the painting is good, the viewer will look for your signature and find it. If it is bad, why blatantly advertise your name?

8 EXERCISES IN LANDSCAPE PAINTING

Clear Skies
Cloudy Skies
Fields, Roads and Mountains
Trees
Shrubs
The Sea
Water and Rocks
Ships and Boats
Human Figures

Camille Pissarro. *Urban Landscape* (detail).

In this chapter we'll study practical applications of landscape painting. Exercises will cover the following topics:

Sky and clouds.

Fields, roads and mountains.

Trees and shrubs.

Rocks, sea and boats.

Figures in the landscape.

CLEAR SKIES

The sky is usually an important part of a landscape painting. Sometimes it occupies more than half the painting.

Many artists have specialized in painting skies. Sisley said, "I always begin my paintings by painting the sky."

A

B

Sky color is always brighter close to the horizon, as figure A shows. Sky color is not always blue. It often has a yellow, red, green or violet hue, as in figure B. It is usually necessary to paint the sky with a variety of colors, using different types of brushstrokes. Break up the pattern of uniformity, as shown in figure C. Figure C is a detail of a patch of sky painted by Camille Pissarro.

C

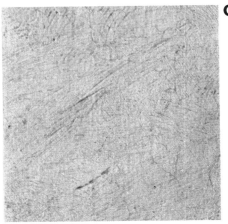

The sky's color and its lightness usually affect color harmony in the painting.

Practice painting skies as often as possible. Paint clear skies, cloudy skies, skies at dawn, dusk and afternoon. Beautiful effects can be produced with a few clouds. The painting's theme can often be the sky itself.

Color is more *intense* at the top of a clear, smooth sky. It usually becomes brighter on the horizon. Blue often has a *reddish cast* in the upper part of the sky. It is often closer to *ultramarine blue* in color. Lower down, near the horizon, blue loses its intensity. It may have a slightly *yellowish hue.*

The illustrations above show differences in sky colors.

Skies must not be painted as a perfectly harmonized blend of color. It would be unreal and mechanical. It would have the appearance of a metallic background.

Try to create a *mixture of light and color.* Mix other blues with the general, overall blue.

Paint with different types of brushstrokes. Alternate bold strokes with soft touches to break up the uniform pattern.

Sky color is *not always blue.* It may be blue with a *yellow, green, pink* or *violet tinge.* It may be *totally* yellow, green, pink or violet without *any* obvious blue.

With this in mind, you can choose a range of warm or cold colors. You can emphasize the color range in the subject, or devise a new range.

CLOUDY SKIES

The preceding principles for painting clear skies also apply to cloudy skies. A cloudy sky usually has a background of blue, pink, green, violet or yellow. Clouds are painted over this background.

Begin painting a cloudy sky by leaving blank spaces for clouds. Paint and shape the clouds later. Figures A and B below show this technique.

In figure A the white spaces are canvas left blank. These spaces can be painted after the sky color has been applied, as in figure B.

A   B

Sunlight falling on drifting clouds creates areas of highlight, reflected light and shadow, as this oil sketch shows.

Clouds are an exercise in draftsmanship and values. Shapes, contrasts, colors, shadows and reflected light are the keys to well-painted clouds. You'll paint floating lumps of cotton balls instead of clouds if you don't pay attention to these factors.

Practice drawing clouds often. Use blue-tinted paper and charcoal. You'll need a small stick of white pastel or conte crayon. Make a blurred pattern with charcoal or crayon. Then draw with the white pastel. Use a kneaded eraser to bring out white patches and outline areas of half-light.

If it isn't convenient to draw direct from Nature, use good photographs. A cloud is a drifting mass lighted by the sun from one direction. Brilliant light falls on areas of the clouds. These areas contrast with the darker background of the sky.

Some areas are in shadow on the unlighted side. Others are covered with patches of reflected light. Figure C above illustrates lighting and shadows in clouds.

Clouds are usually bright white in their sunlit areas. You may need to use the palette knife to paint smooth, flat patches.

Shady parts of cumulus clouds are gray against a blue sky on a sunny day. In such conditions, the shadowy-gray of clouds is brighter than the blue of the sky.

This general principle does not apply to an overcast sky or cloudy sky threatening rain. In rainy skies, cloud color may be a deep gray, darker than the blue or gray of the sky.

FIELDS, ROADS AND MOUNTAINS

Soil colors in fields, roads and mountains change according to the landscape, season and weather.

Earth color is usually dark in cultivated areas, lighter in uncultivated areas. It's lighter still in roads and paths. Here's the reason:

Cultivated soil has clods of different sizes. It's usually damp and has a rough structure that encourages shadow.

Soil of roads and paths is dry and smooth. It reflects more light, so it has a lighter tone. The color and shadows of cultivated earth lean toward sienna and red. The color of roads and paths is yellowish in sunlit parts and bluish in shade. The oil sketch on the opposite page illustrates this coloring.

Earth color is never *uniform*. This is true of fields, roads and meadows, whatever their actual color may be. It's necessary to mix varied colors with the actual color. Observe small differences of color in your subjects. They really are there!

Don't overdo one-color earth patches. A fault of some painters is to mix a blend of paint resembling earth and then paint it everywhere. Remember the following guideline:

> **No two colors of earth are identical.**
> **Study differences between earth tones.**
> **Make them obvious in your painting.**

Be careful with the direction of brushstrokes. They should nearly always be horizontal. A field painted with vertical brushstrokes looks like grass or dry wheat.

Mountains and hills lose their vivid colors and become a mass of blue, violet or gray when they are in the background.

Sometimes mountains or hills are in the middle distance. They may exhibit a variety of earth patches, rocks, vegetation and trees. All will have different shapes and colors.

Don't ignore this variety in your paintings. I have seen many poorly painted landscapes because the artist failed to observe and interpret these differences.

Earth colors appear in many hues, as this sketch shows. Colors A and B correspond to the sunlit and shadowed parts of uncultivated land. Color C is typical of a sunlit path or road. Color D is the road in shadow. Cultivated earth tends toward dark sienna—E. Areas in shadow have a dark color tending toward reddish-blue—F.

Successful drawings and paintings of trees require many hours of sketching and studying tree structure. There are as many tree shapes as there are tree varieties. These drawings illustrate both dead and living trees.

TREES

Shapes and colors of trees shouldn't be haphazardly painted from memory. Painting tree branches and leaves is laborious. It requires steady work and concentration.

The best approach to painting trees is to have *patience*.

Discipline yourself. Spend as much time drawing trees and shrubs as you can. Draw bare trees with just main branches. Then draw groups of branches and branches covered with leaves. Above are some examples.

Figures A and B illustrate two stages in painting trees in the distance. Edges are intentionally left rough and blurry. There are few details. Only patches of color and general shapes are painted.

TREES IN DISTANCE

The tree illustrations above show how to paint trees in the distance. Paint them without sharply defined outlines. Use patches of color without showing small branches and leaves.

Masses are painted as blocks of green in both figures A and B. One block is light green and the other is dark. The areas around the tree are painted in the same loose style, without details.

Next comes the more detailed process of painting a tree in the foreground, as shown in the following exercises. Shapes and colors must be defined in foreground trees. This process is detailed, but not difficult.

C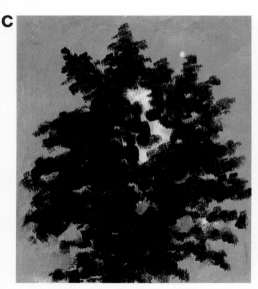

D

Trees in foreground are detailed. The sketch above shows the first stage. The sky is painted around the charcoal drawing, extending into areas of the tree. Then the dark green of the tree is applied.

Problems of volume and construction in the first stage of painting trees can be solved with few colors. Only the three colors below—blue for sky, greenish-black and a bright green—were used to paint this stage.

E

TREES IN FOREGROUND

Let's start an exercise with a tree drawn in charcoal showing light areas, shadows, trunk, branches and leaves. This drawing will serve as a framework. It will later be covered by the first coat of oil paint. It's a preliminary study that outlines problems of volume, contrast and construction.

The steps are shown in figure C above.

Tree Shadows and Sky—Mix sky color of *ultramarine blue* and *white*. Then cover the sky with this paint diluted with essence of turpentine. Extend paint into parts of the drawing that correspond to leaves of the tree.

Next, mix *Prussian blue* and *burnt umber* for the dark tree areas. Add plenty of essence of turpentine. This will give you a dark green that is almost black. If the tree's actual color is a brighter green, then mix the tree color with more Prussian blue. If the tree is dark green overall, add more burnt umber.

Paint the general tree structure with this dark color. Leave free of paint only the sunlit parts and *holes* through which sky can be seen. This completes the first stage.

Adding Form and Volume—I have painted three samples of color in figure E—the blue of the sky, a medium green and the greenish-black of the first stage. Medium green is made of Prussian blue, yellow, yellow ochre and a small quantity of white.

Figure D shows the completed second stage of the tree. Study the function of the medium green paint. Note that I have painted with all three colors together.

I have used greenish-black to create the silhouette of leaves against the blue sky. The medium green represents highlighted areas of the tree. It also defines shapes and groups of leaves.

Last, the blue is painted over holes through which sky can be seen.

Less essence of turpentine is used in the second stage. This allows a thicker medium green paint to cover the dark green.

Finishing Touches—We must now proceed more slowly. Look at the masses in the tree's structure in figure G on page 94. Study the light, shade and colors. Note differences between *luminous* greens, *medium* greens and *shady* greens. Paint these areas with thick pigment.

Usually it is best to paint brighter colors over darker colors. Notice where bright leaves stand out against dark backgrounds.

Paint in bold strokes. Constantly put fresh, clean color on the brush. This is done so color on the brush does not lose its initial hue when applied on other wet colors.

F

Here are some sample colors I mixed while painting the tree in figure G. There are six shades of green, one sienna, one medium blue and one dark blue. Some of these colors—sienna and medium blue—can't be readily seen in the tree. But they were used as parts of mixtures to create shadows and reflections.

G

This finished tree painting shows greater detail, more careful construction and better color. Final color is achieved by application of light colors on darker colors. Care must be taken to make contrasting values.

Don't blend light and dark colors with the brush. Apply them to the canvas with the brush full of paint. Avoid an excess of blends that will blur the shape. Remember that leaves are flat. They are patches of flat color, superimposed on other lighter or darker flat colors.

Work on the sky by thickening and modifying the color. A little Prussian blue and a touch of yellow can be added to the original mixture of ultramarine blue and white. Add some of this new sky color to spaces in the tree.

Colors must be diversified. Don't settle for two or three shades of green and continue painting with them to the end. Try to see all shades and colors of the tree. Try to *accentuate* them. Figure F shows examples of colors I have used to paint this tree.

Figure G shows the finished stage. Blue sky patches have been painted over dark, shady parts of the tree. Blue brushstrokes superimposed on the background help portray the thick and thin branches.

Paint mainly with the darker green and sky blue to establish outlines, construct leaves and make them stand out. Last, paint the more *luminous* masses of leaves.

Squint your eyes to visualize the color scheme as a whole. Do colors combine in a harmonized, coherent range? If not, adjust your colors until you have a pleasing scheme.

SHRUBS

The method of painting shrubs and green fields is similar to painting trees.

Here's an important principle first expressed by Leonardo da Vinci. It is still valid:

In landscapes of similar color values, the green of plants and trees will always be darker than the fields.

The Van Gogh painting on page 55 and the landscape on page 111 illustrate this contrast in values.

THE SEA

Sky color is reflected by the sea. The same is true for lakes and rivers. The following is a fundamental guideline:

If there is a *blue sky*, there will be a *bluish sea*. If there is a *gray sky*, there will be a *grayish sea*.

Sea color is affected by the atmosphere between it and the viewer. Water in the distance is lighter in color than in the foreground. Color contrasts are stronger in the foreground. Foreground details are sharply defined. The background is blurry and less detailed.

Painting wave movement and white foam breaking on the beach requires practice and thorough knowledge of the subject. You must paint from *memory,* because the movement never "freezes." But always paint with reference to the subject before you.

The sea is in constant motion. Wave movement, eddying water near rocks and breaking foam is something we see again and again. Each time it assumes different forms. These forms repeat themselves in similar patterns.

Our task is to observe the sea carefully and remember clearly. Then we can paint from memory.

Sea color is usually blue or blue-green. But a foreground with rocks presents a variety of shades and colors. Colors may vary from black to green and bright blue. They may have gray reflections and flashes of white, or grayish white.

We have to spend a long time looking at that part of the scene where water forms whitecaps. Analyze it thoroughly. Forget the water's movement and try to determine the precise color of that brightness, which probably is not white at all. It is probably a light blue or slightly yellowish green.

Rocks are basically cubes with or without sharp angles. This depends on whether they are dry or washed by waves. They have to be painted with different colors for each different plane. When waves break on rocks, the rocks become darker in tone.

The seascape on the opposite page illustrates guidelines for painting sea and rocks.

Problems are similar in painting the sea, lakes and deep rivers. Reflections in water nearly always represent the mirror image of objects on land or on the water. They are usually in slightly more vivid colors, with shapes broken up by movement of water.

ANALYZING WATER AND ROCKS

Look at the seascape on the opposite page. This is a detail from my painting titled *Costa Brava*. Let's analyze six parts of this painting. Numbers correspond to parts of the painting.

1—Compare color of the sea in contrast with rocks in the distance. Note color and contrast of rocks in the distance and foreground. Outlines are more blurred and color is lighter and less intense in the distance. Color of the sea is lighter in the distance than in the foreground.

2—The waterline on the rocks is shown as a dark line. This line is conspicuous because it is here that waves break and produce white foam. Keep this in mind when painting rocks at the water's edge.

3—Note the angular shape of rocks in this small outcrop in the center. The rocks are basically cubes. Try to accentuate shapes by painting boldly. Rocks are made dramatic by light and shade. Even in shaded parts of rocks there are various colors and reflected light.

4—When rocks are near the water's edge, they lose their sharp angles and edges. This is caused by continuous erosion by waves.

5—Observe how water breaks against rocks to form bluish-white foam. The foam has been painted on a dark surface using white, light blue and gray with a few brushstrokes.

6—Color of water in the foreground varies from almost black to green and bluish tones. It's not difficult to paint the color of water as long as you ignore your *preconceived notions* of color. Water is not always *blue*. Paint what you see in the subject, without any distractions.

J.M. Parramon. *Costa Brava* (detail).

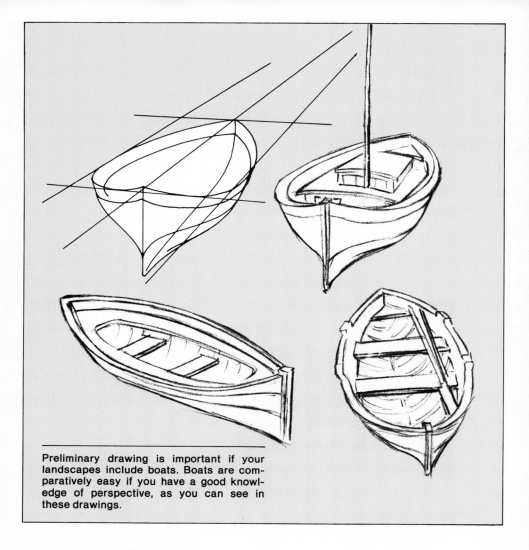

Preliminary drawing is important if your landscapes include boats. Boats are comparatively easy if you have a good knowledge of perspective, as you can see in these drawings.

SHIPS AND BOATS

Portraying *structure* is the fundamental problem in painting ships and boats. Make careful preliminary drawings, such as those shown above.

Color of ships and boats is usually vivid and brilliant. This is especially true in bright sunlight. The subject lends itself to emphasizing contrast of light and shade. Complementary colors can often be used.

At sea and in harbor, there may be considerable contrast of colors between middle distance and background. This is an example of how atmosphere affects the finished painting.

Camille Pissarro. *Urban Landscape.*

This close-up detail of Pissarro's painting shows an enlarged figure. Note how its dimensions correspond to the correct proportions of a human body. The artist has used an extraordinary variety of shapes and colors.

HUMAN FIGURES IN LANDSCAPES

Landscape paintings of open country, urban scenes, coastal areas and mountains often include human figures. Including figures adds human interest to the landscape.

The Impressionists were highly skilled draftsmen as well as excellent painters. Drawing was a basis for their success. Good drawing—even simple outlines such as this one—is essential for good painting.

Make many sketches of figures as preliminary exercises. This gives the artist knowledge and skill needed to paint the picture. Sketches express shapes and masses in a few lines or brushstrokes. Sketching cultivates the ability to see and interpret color.

The Impressionists wanted to portray live, natural scenes. They painted hundreds of paintings with human figures in them. Many have only small figures.

Look at Camille Pissarro's *Urban Landscape* on page 99.

Proportions of human figures are correct. If we could enlarge figures enough to analyze them, we would see that their heads, waists, arms and legs are in proportion to their height. Proper proportions hold true in spite of their small relative size in the painting.

Heads of figures are drawn with one or two brushstrokes. Three or four brushstrokes give shape to the body and a few more to skirts or trousers.

They are an accurate reflection of human figures. The painter must observe and study them like waves of the sea, retaining in his memory their stationary postures.

Colors can be changed or locations of figures can be altered for compositional purposes. Use this artistic license to best advantage for contrast, focus of attention and dramatizing surroundings.

Direct Painting
Attitude
Sketching
Direct Painting in a
Single Session
Direct Painting in
Several Sessions
Painting with the
Palette Knife

J.M. Parramon. _La Mota_ (detail).

Van Gogh painted more than 800 landscapes and completed as many drawings in the last two years of his life. One of his biographers, Irving Stone, said that Van Gogh painted from 4 a.m. until nightfall. He painted two or three paintings per day.

Van Gogh and the majority of the Impressionists began and finished their landscapes in one uninterrupted session. They introduced the technique known as _direct painting_. They believed they should paint the _impression of the moment_. This was in contrast to the technique of painting by stages, which had predominated for centuries.

Direct Painting

In _direct painting,_ the artist paints according to a well-defined plan from the first moment.

Camille Corot said, "I know from experience that it is very useful to begin by sketching the painting in simple terms. Paint step by step, as completely as possible, following your first intentions. Very little remains to be done once you have covered the entire canvas. I have found that all that is carried out directly turns out more natural and more agreeable. When we do this we benefit from the possibility of a happy accident."

Corot's remarks give us an important principle we can follow:

> **Paint with a well-defined plan
> from the first moment.**

Following this principle depends on experience and skill. It also depends on the *psychological attitude* of the artist toward painting.

ATTITUDE

Attitude is very important to painting. Here's why:

When we paint we rarely employ our full intellectual capacity. We normally work with a certain degree of mental idleness, without full concentration.

We may paint without wholehearted commitment. We take it for granted that there is always a second time to repaint. We know we can have second thoughts and correct our work.

But we *can't* have second thoughts if we are to paint directly.

The technique of direct painting involves a different attitude. We must remember there will be only one chance to resolve problems. We must have self-discipline to leave alone what is first painted.

We have to be bold enough to paint with broad brushstrokes, with the brush full of paint. We must act on our first impressions. We have to be committed fully from beginning to end of the painting.

The results will be *freshness* and *originality* in our finished work.

SKETCHING

The sketch is a small painting made as a *rough draft.* A color sketch can be painted on cardboard, sometimes in less than an hour. It's a typical example of direct final plan for painting.

Sketching is also an excellent example of expressing originality. The sketch is the painting already *seen* and *painted,* at least in rough form. The sketch is a preliminary effort that commits us to the final plan for painting.

J.M. Parramon. *La Mota.* This oil landscape was done in the technique of direct painting in a single session. It took an hour and 10 minutes. The blurred outlines and blank, unpainted parts of canvas are evidence of the rapid painting period. Note the rough, unfinished upper right portion of sky. In this type of painting there is no *preliminary sketch.* Direct painting in a single session is itself a type of sketching.

The landscape above shows a color sketch that I painted to illustrate this idea.

The following are notes I took when I painted this sketch:

I begin by applying blue-gray to the mountain in the left background. Using the same color and same brush, I draw the outline of the cypresses, church tower and houses. I also draw lines that constitute edges of the foreground.

With the same color, but a bit darker, I paint shadows of the church tower and house. Next I paint the shape of the mountain behind them.

Now I change brush and color to paint the dark green of the cypresses. I fill in dark parts of edges of fields and meadows.

Another brush with green color for meadows.

Now the sky with a new brush, and a color mixed of ultramarine blue, white and a touch of yellow.

Working carefully, I blend color for sunlit portions of buildings.

Now for the reddish color of the roofs, adding alizarin crimson and white to the luminous color of the houses.

Next, I clean the brush of blue-gray color I first used. Then I blend a darker color — viridian, alizarin crimson, burnt sienna and yellow ochre. I use this to construct and paint dark portions of edges in the foreground.

Viridian and ochre are used for sunlit parts of cypresses.

Then bluish-gray for trees and shadows of houses.

The notes end with a final remark — *Time: one hour and 10 minutes.*

It isn't possible to give more specific details, because I was painting directly. From the first brushstroke I had a deliberate attitude.

I began by painting a hill and — with the same color — drawing the outline of cypresses, church tower and houses. All this was done with an attitude of *seeing everything at once* and *not hesitating.*

The Impressionists painted in a similar manner. They concentrated their energy in a few sessions of frenzied effort. They committed themselves to the subject, to the color and to the painting.

A good example of this development can be seen in the work of Cézanne. After painting in more than one sitting, Cézanne decided to complete many of his paintings in one session. He treated them as sketches, as shown in figure A on the opposite page.

Cézanne later painted in an almost abstract style. He produced works in which shapes and colors were vividly expressed.

In figure B opposite, we see a reproduction of Cézanne's *Mont Saint-Victoire.* It was painted directly with independent brushstrokes. The strokes do not cover the entire canvas. We can also see in this painting the beginnings of the *Cubist style,* of which Cézanne was a forerunner.

A

Paul Cézanne. *The Black Castle.* Cézanne's famous painting, *The House of the Hanged Man*—reproduced on page 41—is known as a masterpiece. It was done in 1872, the first year in which Cézanne painted according to Impressionist principles. It was a carefully planned work, painted in two or more sessions. Thirty years later, Cézanne's style had matured. His search for simplicity had led him to paint pictures such as this one. This landscape was completed in one sitting. It is painted in the style and with the finish of a color sketch.

B

Paul Cézanne. *Mont Saint-Victoire.* Cézanne reached full development of his style with this landscape. It was painted during the period 1901-1906. His landscapes show a pattern of almost abstract shapes. His brushstrokes are broad and flat. He reduces objects, trees and houses to basic shapes. This painting contains the beginnings of Cubism. Cézanne merely puts *colors* on canvas. He paints a picture with extraordinary speed at a single sitting. In this work he deliberately left blank, unpainted spaces on the canvas.

Direct Painting in a Single Session _____

The following painting exercises were done to illustrate the method of direct painting in a single session. As in the preceding exercise, I kept notes to explain the techniques used in each step. Let's follow the progress.

The subject chosen for this study is a mountain landscape with a wide range of fields, meadows, trees and vegetation. It is 3:30 p.m.

First, I set up the easel and prepare palette and brushes. The illustrations on the opposite page and page 108 show distribution of colors on the palette and how to hold palette and brushes.

INTERPRETATION

The subject is magnificent. Its qualities are evident in the color photograph on the opposite page. The photograph was taken during morning hours. I think it has a potentially monotonous effect because of repetitious shapes and colors.

There are many trees, all of similar shape and color. Fields present a similar color range. This is especially true in the upper part of the painting where field and trees blend into a neutral mass. This area is blue-gray-green in color.

I decide to confine myself to the area that offers greatest variety. I will emphasize that variety, making meadows and fields more sharply defined. I will differentiate colors, eliminating or bringing together groups of trees.

Finally, I will establish distances between them, letting the meadows be seen more easily.

The horizon is almost at the top of the painting with two hills in the background. There is an outline where different strips of land begin, almost without trees.

Groups of trees and shrubs are more sharply defined in the bottom half of the painting. There is a meadow in the foreground.

Now I begin the first stage.

This is the expansive landscape chosen for an exercise in direct painting in a single session.

It's a good habit to put colors on the palette in a definite order. This photograph shows a good arrangement. Starting at upper right—white, followed by yellow, yellow ochre, dark umber, vermilion, alizarin crimson, viridian, cobalt blue, ultramarine blue and Prussian blue.

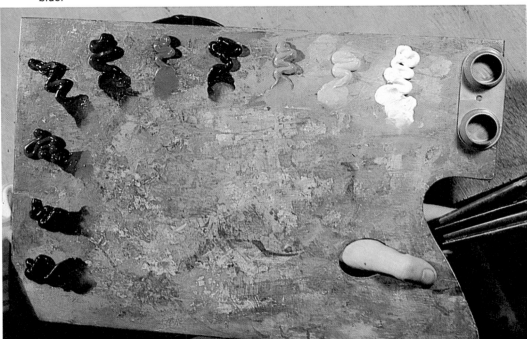

1—If you paint right-handed, hold the palette, brushes and rag in your left hand. If you paint left-handed, do the opposite. Brushes are held by pressing them against the underside edge of the palette. Spread them out in a fan-shape. Then they won't touch each other and mix paints.

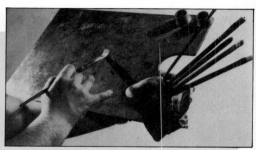

2—Hold the brush in your painting hand as if it were a pencil—but closer to the handle's end. Your thumb helps to keep the palette steady, but its real support is your forearm. Let it rest on your arm, using your thumb as a lever. Holding and supporting the palette continuously is tiring and painful. Some artists leave the palette on the painting box or a table.

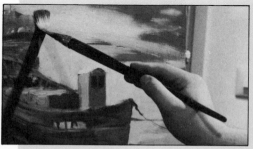

3—This is the usual way of painting with the brush. Holding it near the end makes it possible to leave distance between each brushstroke. It also allows a better view of the painting surface.

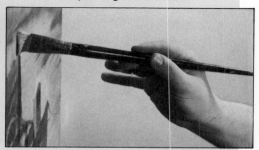

4—The brush is held here in position for horizontal brushstrokes. You have to turn your hand slightly and make the brushstrokes from side to side. Experiment with a variety of painting positions.

5—This is another useful way to hold the brush. The brush handle is held in your hand as you would hold a sword, with your forefinger extended slightly. The brush is controlled mainly by your thumb and forefinger. This makes it possible to paint with your arm fully extended. You have greater freedom and ease of movement with broad brushstrokes. This technique gives you a wider view of the picture.

6—An experienced painter occasionally leans slightly backward from the waist. He stretches out his arm and squints his eyes. This pose may appear awkward. But it arises from the need to visualize masses and colors, and to paint from a distance.

This is the first stage showing my interpretation.

FIRST STAGE—CONSTRUCTION

Flat No. 4 and No. 6 brushes are used in the first stage shown above. I use the *edge* of the No. 4 for fine brushstrokes and the *flat side* for broad strokes. I use the No. 6 for larger areas of trees and shrubs.

Next, I mix Prussian blue and burnt umber with a small amount of yellow ochre. Colors are mixed with a large quantity of essence of turpentine. They are almost liquid, which allows them to dry faster.

Sometimes I paint with my *fingers,* rubbing paint in to achieve *transparent* tones. They look like patches of watercolor or smears of pastels.

I work slowly, studying the painting carefully before applying each brushstroke. I calculate the exact location of each line and shape. I paint without hesitation, trying not to lose my smooth *rhythm.* I attempt to construct the painting spontaneously.

Soon, the first stage is complete.

Second stage showing background colors.

SECOND STAGE—APPLYING COLOR

It is now 4:15 p.m. I have been working 45 minutes. There is still plenty of light. But the range of colors is no longer greenish-blue as it was this morning. The landscape now has a yellow ochre hue.

To begin, I will paint with a warm range of green colors. On the palette I mix several shades of green that have a tendency toward yellow ochre, yellow and sienna. Using four brushes, I cover the surface quickly with fairly thin paint.

Later, I may go back over them, depending on whether the tones I use are satisfactory.

At this stage I must be careful. I have to follow the initial structure, limitations and shapes of preliminary lines.

Painting steadily, I put color on dark areas and cover tree shadows with a thicker coat. Later, I will make trees and shadows stand out against the background.

Final stage showing finishing touches.

FINAL STAGE—
ADJUSTING COLORS AND FINISHING TOUCHES

It is now 4:30 p.m. It has taken an hour to reach the final stage. Now I mix thick paints in specific colors. It's as if the painting were *really* beginning now.

I paint colors with easy brushstrokes starting at the top. There are greens, ochres, browns, blue-greens and pinks. I paint dark portions with other brushes.

Now I begin painting lines of trees and shrubs in the middle distance and background.

Next, meadows and trees are painted in the lower half of the painting, using larger brushes.

Colors applied in the second stage serve as a background and foundation for this final stage. They make it possible to complete the initial concept of the scene.

My first intention has been guiding me. I have always kept the following four fundamental factors in mind while painting:

Summarize mentally what impressions you get from the subject.

Paint directly without hesitation. What is done, is done.

Use a diversity of colors.

Paint in the right direction— *horizontal* for meadows and fields, *vertical* for trees and shrubs.

Now the painting is finished. It's 5:30 p.m. This single session of painting has taken two hours.

Direct Painting in Several Sessions

Now let's examine the method of painting directly in more than one session.

The subject is a landscape with green mountains in the background. Buildings and a church tower are in the middle distance. Yellow ochre fields make up the foreground. This scene is pictured on page 20.

The landscape is drawn in charcoal during the first session. I study the composition and make an interpretation. There will be a *second stage* as part of this first session.

In the second stage, I'll paint with thin colors well-diluted with essence of turpentine. I'll leave general adjustments and finishing touches until the following day.

**FIRST STAGE—
COMPOSITION, INTERPRETATION AND DRAWING**

Figure B on the opposite page shows how I have emphasized the Golden Section Principle. The line coincides with the outline of the hill on which buildings and church tower are located.

This shows completion of the first stage of composition, interpretation and construction. Drawing medium was mainly charcoal during the first stage.

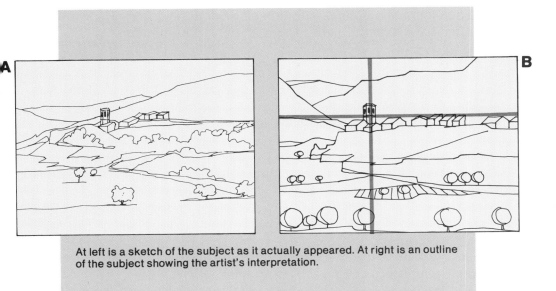

At left is a sketch of the subject as it actually appeared. At right is an outline of the subject showing the artist's interpretation.

I place buildings in an arbitrary, almost horizontal line. I change the shape and height of mountains in the background. They now have more importance because of increased size.

The church tower and buildings stand out in *stronger contrast* against a more ample background. I reduce the length of the small hill on the left side. I emphasize horizontal lines dividing yellow meadows in the foreground.

Finally, I draw fields with crops painted in straight lines that do not exist in the real model. I place trees in the meadow where I want to vary that part of the painting.

This interpretation required unusual persistence. I repeatedly revised my early ideas to reach the end of this first stage.

This is an advantage of painting directly in more than one session. It allows more time to plan and paint without rushing. I have been able to erase parts of the charcoal drawing and redraw features. Charcoal is easily erased with cloth.

Structure of the painting is established. I *fix* the drawing with a special aerosol spray, called *fixative.*

Then I go over all lines with thin oil paint diluted in essence of turpentine. I use a mixture of Prussian blue and burnt umber.

This procedure further establishes structure with broad brushstrokes. The brushstrokes show throughout later stages of painting, some even in the finished work.

SECOND STAGE—
HARMONIZING COLORS

Now I begin painting with thin coats of color. This will be the base for the final session. I paint large and small spaces. I do not yet include details or definite shapes.

I begin with sky and mountains. Then I paint the small hill on which the buildings are located. I continue with the yellow and earth colors of the meadow.

Buildings and trees are left until last so I can more easily determine their final colors. It is easier to determine colors and values of some shapes when larger color areas are painted first.

Above is the completed second stage. Work done so far makes it possible to anticipate the final result—range of colors, contrast and composition. Thin paint was used here. It dries quickly and makes it possible to finish the picture at a second sitting.

Two general principles are important to remember when *beginning* a painting:

Begin by painting large areas first to *fill* space. This eliminates the influence of white canvas. Leave white areas of canvas where appropriate.

Paint darker areas before lighter areas, especially those colors contrasting strongly with the white canvas. Then paint smaller and lighter areas. This helps adjust color contrasts.

Paint in broad strokes without blending colors during the early stage. This improves shapes and colors of objects. The technique is similar to Cézanne's methods in his last years.

Painting with flat brushstrokes forces us to visualize the painting as a whole. We paint with fewer strokes. It leads to a modern, impressionistic interpretation of the subject.

Now decide on the *color range*.

The initial process of filling the canvas with colors does not mean I can paint without concern for color harmony. I can't assume that I can repaint and adjust colors during the second session. This is incorrect.

Color harmony is decided in the first session. I must paint and visualize the painting as a whole. I'm not obliged to include small details.

I imagine a range of warm colors with this subject. I put more yellow, more ochre, more sienna and red on the palette thinking these colors will be dominant in the final painting.

This session required two hours of drawing and painting until I completed the first stage. I will begin the final session in two days.

FINAL SESSION

It is time for overall adjustment and finishing touches. The end result is shown on the opposite page.

Colors painted during the first stage two days earlier are virtually dry. Now it is possible to easily paint over them.

First, I emphasize outlines of shapes. I use a dark color based on Prussian blue and burnt umber to bring out shapes of the church tower and building roofs. I use the same color to outline trees, shrubs and roads at the bottom of the hill.

Next, I adjust color and shapes of the background hills. I emphasize differences in elevation and sudden slopes and dips.

Now, I adjust the shape and color of the mountain on the left. There are bright and dark patches under the luminous green.

Then I clean the palette. I prepare a range of green colors to paint trees below the hill where buildings are located.

I work with thick paint, painting from dark to light. I superimpose colors that reflect light on green colors in shadow.

Above is the completed painting. It was done in two sessions—one of two hours and a second of three hours. Most of the picture was painted during the second session. The final work was based on the rougher painting done during the first session.

It is necessary to use broader brushes, No. 6 and No. 8. This prevents me from painting with excessive detail. I try to avoid smooth blends and transitions that can lead to a *soft* and *overworked* painting.

Now I clean the palette and brushes and put on new colors.

Next, I mix pigment to repaint and adjust colors of the buildings and church tower. I see that there are two identical colors in the light and shade of the buildings. I try to accentuate differences.

Occasionally I squint my eyes to see masses of color better. There is contrast in sunlit walls against the background of mountain shadows. Shadows are blue-green.

I try to emphasize this luminous effect by enhancing contrasts and accentuating darker parts of mountains where they join walls and roofs of buildings.

Using ochre, yellow and reddish colors, I paint earth shades of roads and outlines of the hill.

Now I return to trees on the small hill. I modify and darken some highly sunlit areas that are excessively bright. They seem to clash with bright colors of the buildings.

Next, I paint trees in the meadow and the earth-colored edges. I emphasize lines dividing fields. Again I clean the palette and brushes and apply new colors.

I paint fields of wheat with mixtures of yellow and ochre with white and a small amount of red. I paint shadows cast by hills over the yellow fields. Then I turn my attention once more to the sky, repainting it with thicker paint and correcting colors.

Again, I clean the palette and brushes. Now I go back to the buildings and paint windows and doors. I continue painting parts of mountains, chimneys of buildings and trees on the small hill at left.

I draw furrows in the middle fields with the brush handle, using it like a pencil. I further modify colors of the church tower's shadow and sunlit walls.

Three hours have been spent in the second painting session. I will leave it. I think I have finished. It will be easier to judge tomorrow. If necessary, I can retouch the painting.

Here are some hints on painting during the second session.

Clean Palette and Brushes. Apply New Colors—This is an elementary and mechanical procedure. It is important for success in painting. Cleaning the palette and brushes frequently allows a fresh range of colors. It means creating a fresh attitude and starting again without color mixtures that may turn gray. Don't neglect to mix clean, fresh colors.

Paint in All Parts of the Painting—During the second session it is helpful to paint randomly in various places on the canvas. Paint trees, then buildings, then trees again, then sky. Move around as if "walking about in the painting." Paint in a carefree manner without stopping in any particular place. This helps avoid painting and repainting the scene until you forget what you really want to paint.

Adjustment of Color Sometimes Modifies Nearby Colors—You may decide that a background color should be bluer. When you adjust the blue color you will modify adjacent colors. This is called the *principle of simultaneous contrasts*. When colors are painted next to one another, one may make the other appear *brighter* or *duller*. This principle is important when choosing color schemes.

Remember Your Original Interpretation—Maintain your established concept of the subject when you begin to paint in the second session. Don't become absorbed by the scene. Pause from time to time. Stop painting and look over the work already done. If you find that *your* painting is disappearing and that the *real* scene is dominating, then leave the painting alone. Take it home and finish it later.

Painting with the Palette Knife

The palette knife can be an interesting substitute or replacement for the brush.

Landscape painting with the palette knife was first done by Gustave Courbet in the middle of the 19th century. Most of the Impressionist painters experimented with this method. They found it a way to modernize the style of their work.

The *richness* and *brilliance* of oil paints applied with the palette knife inspired the Fauvists to paint many works using this instrument.

The drawings below illustrate three types of palette knives.

Palette knives for painting are usually in the shape of a stonemason's trowel.

Three types of palette knives used in oil painting are the butter knife shape at left, straight trowel at center and bent trowel, right. The trowel knives—especially the bent type—are most commonly used for painting and cleanup. The butter knife-shaped tool is used for cleaning palettes after painting.

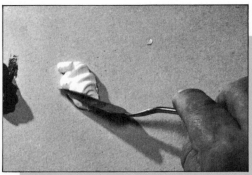

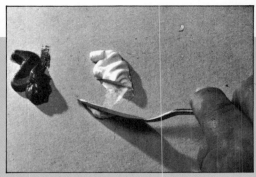

1—Hold the palette knife in this position to pick up paint. Cut the paint with the edge of the knife.

2—Slide the desired amount of paint away from the main portion. Keep this bit of paint clean—don't let other paint mix with it at this stage.

3—You can hold the paint on your knife while you study your painting. It will stick to the knife until you are ready to paint with it. If you are going to mix this paint with another color, go to step 4.

4—Spread the paint on the palette. Press it into a paste.

PAINTING TECHNIQUES

Don't use thinners when painting with a palette knife. Colors are mixed and applied undiluted as they come from the tube. The palette knife is used for mixing pigment and collecting it on the palette.

Work with a maximum of three or four palette knives of different shapes. They have blades of different sizes.

The series of photographs above shows how to use the palette knife to pick up oil paint, spread it as a paste, mix it, and then paint with it.

5—Now you can mix another color with the first. Take the second color and spread it on the first. Mix them together as you would use a fork to beat eggs. Collect the new paint mixture into a pile when it spreads out too much on the palette. Then mix it and press it again.

6—Now the pigment is mixed and ready for painting. Cut a portion of paint from the palette with the knife as in step 1. Apply paint to the canvas in the same manner as shown in steps 3 and 4.

7—Use the palette knife to cut and trim paint on the canvas, outlining and drawing shapes.

8—If you prefer, colors can be applied on top of each other and mixed directly on the canvas as you paint.

TWO EFFECTIVE METHODS

Palette knives can be used *directly* or on *quick sketches* made with thin paint.

Both procedures can be summarized as follows:

Painting Over Thin Paint—The first stage consists of painting with brushes. Use oil paint well-diluted with essence of turpentine. Thin colors lend a hue to the canvas but do not result in a thick coat of paint.

On top of this preliminary thin coat, apply paint with the palette knife. Mix paint on the canvas or on the palette.

Paint backgrounds and large areas with one operation of the palette knife. Leave the finishing touches for more complex and smaller areas until later stages.

Apply the finishing touches with sable brushes.

There is a difference between painting on a surface of thin paint and painting on blank canvas. In the first case there is background and general harmony of colors. Thin background colors show until covered.

This background enables you to fill in areas and resolve problems on parts where the palette knife has not been used. You can't do this painting on blank canvas.

Painting Directly on Canvas—Mixing colors on the canvas—rather than on the palette—results in a contemporary look. Large areas should be painted in one operation during the first stage. Avoid retouching them during subsequent stages so the initial *spontaneity* is preserved.

Areas with small, complex shapes should be painted with thin paint during the first stage. This makes it possible to emphasize colors and paint on top of them during later stages.

In smaller areas, it is preferable to apply colors already mixed on the palette. But when possible, mix directly on canvas.

Apply finishing touches with a sable brush. Don't destroy the smooth, enameled appearance produced by the palette knife.

This system is especially difficult. It is not advisable for the inexperienced artist. Save it until you have a good command of oil painting with brushes.

USE THE DIRECT METHOD

Painting with the palette knife should be done in the *direct method* in a single session. Start and finish in one operation. This procedure is not suitable for large paintings or for laborious, complex subjects.

This landscape was painted with a palette knife. It illustrates the loose style of the knife technique. Note the richness of color produced by strokes of the knife.

Cézanne painted portraits with the palette knife. But they were not detailed and elaborate portraits like those of Jean-Auguste Dominique Ingres. Cézanne's were really sketches—almost outlines—in which he built up the portrait. He used the edge and flat surface of the palette knife.

The landscape above shows one of my color sketches painted with the palette knife. I painted directly on canvas.

You can see the thick pigment and rough characteristics of painting done with the palette knife. Notice how colors were mixed on the surface to produce mottled hues and irregular blends.

These methods were combined with the technique of painting in *blurred outline.* This produces an appearance that is *simple* and *primitive.*

Finally, analyze the composition. It has been achieved by building up the painting in planes. The color scheme was mixed from unequal proportions of complementary colors.

ON WITH PAINTING

Now you have information to help you paint landscapes.

The success of your painting depends partly on the amount of time you can devote to it.

The writer Francis Jourdain once asked Cézanne, "If a young painter asked your advice, what would you say to him?"

Cézanne answered, "I would tell him to develop his skill, to draw a great deal, to copy and copy and recopy the pipe of his stove until he gets it exactly right. Only then will he be in a position to talk about painting."

Courbet said that *every artist must be his own teacher.*

Now you have the information to be just that.

Andre Derain. *View of Martigues.*